Version 19 - Monday, November 14, 2022

NOTE: This book was originally written as a screenplay. This helps to explain why the book includes song titles. The Soundtrack is available to stream on your electronic device, directly from my website: DennyMagicc1.com, at no charge.

This soundtrack was composed by Tom Rae – (Dunoon, Scotland)

Table of Contents

#1 – "Once there was hope"

Suburbia, USA

A residential street with several upper middle class ranch-style homes. All are landscaped nicely, and we can see by the relative age of the trees that line the street that the neighborhood is about ten or more years old.

A late model car approaches, turns into the driveway of one of the homes. The driver parks next to a station wagon. A young executive (Paul Regis) gets out, grabs his coat and briefcase from the back seat, and enters the house.

Paul sets his coat 0n a chair and his briefcase on a small table. Paul yells out, ***"Karen?".*** A female's voice comes from the kitchen, in the rear of the home. It's Paul's wife (Karen Regis) who answers, ***"In here honey!"***

Paul smiles and walks towards the kitchen. As he enters; Paul can see that Karen is busy packing her lunch. She's dressed in a nurse's uniform and appears pressed for time. She turns, walks over to Paul with an open face sandwich in one hand and a butter knife in the other. She, smiles and kisses him on the cheek before responding, ***"Hi lover, what's new?".***

She walks back to the counter where she was working, and she resumes her task. Paul takes a seat at the kitchen table. Then he tries to answer her question, **"Well…".** He pauses, ***"Looks like the Goddard case is going to the appeals court."***

Karen stops working and turns towards Paul sympathetically. She asks, ***"Guess that's bad news, huh?"***

Paul is deep in thought; going over the events of his day when he answers, ***"Well, probably not. We still won the case, but if it goes to appeal we may only be able to get Goddard around 60% of the financial restitution that we were seeking."*** He pauses.

"Instead of 1.5 million. The judgement would only amount to somewhere around nine hundred K.

The biggest problem is that Godard is hinting that he wants to appeal. I mean, we got him the judgement that he originally asked for, but now he's starting to act a little bit greedy." He pauses. ***"I don't think the firm wants to go through another trial. Too damned expensive for everyone concerned."***

Karen asks***, "Can he do that?"***

Paul seems a bit surprised and asks, ***"Who?"***

Karen repeats herself, ***"Goddard. Can he force your firm to file an appeal?"***

Paul answers***, "Sure. He's the plaintiff. He can do anything he wants. But our collective***

opinion is that he should be satisfied with the judgement that we won."

Paul thinking silently to himself for a moment before continuing. ***"Some of these people are suit happy, you know. I mean, he won the damn case and he made out like a bandit already. That's why we filed for a million five in the first place."*** He pauses. ***"Our strategy was to walk with approximately a million, and it worked out great! But now this Bozo wants more, I don't get it."***

Paul is shaking his head. Karen finishes packing her lunch, and as she walks past Paul, she leans over and kisses him on his cheek. She smiles and says, ***"Oh well... I know everything will work itself out honey. It always does, right?"***

Paul smiles, as Karen heads for the front door. She adds, ***"I've got to run, so I'll see you in the witching hours."***

Karen makes her way towards the front door. But before she slams the front door behind her, she adds, ***"Oh, there's a pot roast in the oven, and some baked potatoes. Be sure to eat something before you veg out in front of the TV."***

Paul slips back into thinking about the Godard case, when he suddenly realizes that Karen is off to work. He tries to get her attention before the door slams shut, ***"Hey! I thought you were off graveyard this week."***

Karen stops; she reopens the front door to address Paul. ***"I'm trading shifts with Louise so we can go to that party tomorrow night."*** Then she slams the front door gain and disappears into the couple's driveway.

Paul looks bewildered and speaks out loud to himself. ***"Party? What party?"***

Paul hears Karen's car start as she pulls out of the driveway. He walks down the hallway and re-enters the kitchen. He opens the oven door and smells the pot roast that his wife has affectionately prepared. He speaks to himself out loud. ***"Ummmm, you out did yourself, lover!"***

Paul walks over to a small radio sitting on the window sill and turns on some classical music, then he moves to the back door. He opens it and calls out his dog's name. ***"Panda? Come here boy."***

We see a big Golden Retriever run into the kitchen and he knocks Paul playfully to the floor. Paul obviously loves his pet and is amused by the creature's enthusiasm. He pauses to wrestle with him, doing his best imitation of Humphrey Bogart. ***"Well, I guess it's just you and me sweed-heart [sic]."*** We watch the two of them playing, Paul is laughing as he loses his thoughts of work related annoyances.

Paul's Study - Later that evening

Paul is seen working on some paperwork, he has his reading glasses on and is deep in thought. During this time, we begin to hear noises off in the distance. The sounds [at first] become louder, then they seem to fade away, and then they become louder again.

Paul is finally aware that he is hearing 'something', and he stops working for a moment straining to decipher what the hell it is. He removes his reading glasses and listens intently.

In a moment, after not being able to identify the noises, he resumes his work. A few moments later Panda (his dog), lifts his head and lets out a low-level bark, in the direction of the hallway. Paul looks up, removes his glasses, and speaks to Panda. ***"You hear something boy?"***

Panda gets up off the floor and slowly walks over to Paul's side, he sits down and stares at the hallway, directing his full attention towards the open doorway towards the hall, he lets out a little growl, and another small bark.

Paul stands, walks into the hallway, and leans on the railing looking down at the living room. He strains to identify the noises. It sounds like people moaning, but Paul isn't sure. Although curious, he is also a little nervous and moves cautiously to the head of the stairs. Panda hears it again, and rushes past Paul, down the stairs and into the kitchen. Paul calls out to him just as his tail disappears around the corner, as Panda heads for the kitchen. Paul yells, ***"Panda? PANDA!"***.

Paul descends the stairs following the anxious animal. He makes his way towards the light coming from the kitchen, we hear the sounds a little more clearly now.

The small light above the stove is the only light on. As Paul enters the room he finds Panda sitting on the floor directly in front of the small radio on the window sill, which Paul has left on.

The radio station has since left the air, hours before... and now the radio is only broadcasting the low hiss of static. Paul shakes his head and laughs at himself, thinking that the sounds he was so concerned about probably came from that radio. As he crosses the room to shut it off, Paul notices something odd about the reflection in the window glass above the kitchen sink.

He strains to focus on the image in the glass and becomes frightened at what he sees! The reflection is NOT of his kitchen, but rather, the inside of a prison cell.

Inside are several people, crying out as they reach through the bars. All of them are dressed in tattered uniforms, and all of them have shaved heads.

Paul turns himself around to confront the reflection, only to find his normal kitchen.

The silence is broken by the loud ringing of the kitchen phone which gives Paul a start, causing his heart to race. Paul lets out a gasp, realizes it's only the telephone, and clutching his chest he finally seems to catch his breath. He crosses the room and picks up the receiver. ***"Hello?"***

It's his wife. ***"Hi, Sweetheart. I hope I didn't wake you."***

Paul answers, ***"Uh, no, no... I was going to wait up for you anyway."***

Karen says, ***"Well that's silly. You need to get some rest!"*** Paul sounds a little shaken and Karen senses this, so she asks, ***"Is everything all right, honey?"***

Paul tries to put on a brave face, ***"Oh, yeah, sure. Everything's fine."***

Karen pauses for a moment, then returns to her bubbly self. ***"Well, the reason I called is, I'm going to work a couple of hours overtime, so I should be home around 3 or 3:30 am, so please don't wait up. Ok, Babe?"***

Hospital Corridor - Karen's Workplace

Karen is standing at the counter to one of the hospital's nursing stations. She carefully hands the received across the counter to a nurse who is seated behind it.

The second nurse takes the receiver from Karen's hand and hangs up on her behalf. A co-worker and a friend of Karen's approaches. Anna Johnson, looking very concerned, places a friendly hand on Karen's shoulder. She asks, ***"Problems, Sugar?"***

Karen's frown turns to an accommodating smile as she looks back at Anna. She tries to explain, ***"No, no. It's just that my husband's been wrapped up in a lengthy civil suit for his law firm. He's been burning the candle at both ends."*** Anna smiles and nods. Karen continues her explanation, ***"I think he's been working too hard lately, that's all. I'm just a bit worried about him."***

Anna offers some friendly advice, ***"Maybe he just needs some more loving. You've been putting in a lot of hours yourself lately!"***

Karen feeling a little bit guilty responds, ***"Yea, I should cut back my hours a little..."*** She pauses as if considering that thought. Then she adds, ***"Sure, why not?"***

Anna smiles and adds, ***"That's the spirit, sweetcakes! You just need to roll together in somebody's hay loft!"***

Karen laughs at Anna's suggestion and gives her a gentle shove. Then she sarcastically asks, ***"Is that ALL, you think about?"***

Anna smiles and walks down the hallway. She cranes her neck around to respond, ***"Hey, I'm a sex machine, baby!"***

The Regis Kitchen

Back in the Regis' kitchen. Paul hangs up but has not let go of the telephone receiver yet, as he stares in silence at the empty kitchen.

He slowly walks over to the radio making sure it's turned off. Then he takes a second cautious look out the Kitchen window. Everything is normal.

He turns and looks the entire room over once again. He shakes his head and smiles at his inner fears, then he looks at Panda. ***"Come on, great watchdog of the north, let's hit the sack."*** As the two of them leave the kitchen, Paul shuts off the lights.

Once in the master bedroom, Paul begin to disrobe. He stretches and moves towards the bathroom for a quick shower. He opens the glass shower doors and steps back into the room, stripping off his remaining clothes.

Then he turns reaches over and turns on the water, testing the temperature with the back of his hand. As he retracts his hand from the flow of the water, we again hear the faint voices of moaning people in the distance. Paul stops what he's doing, to listen.

He hears the sounds and is somewhat disturbed, especially after his experience in the kitchen. His heart begins beat rapidly and he begins to breath heavily as he once again, strains to try and make out what those sounds are.

Then as quickly as they showed up, they stop. Paul finally begins to relax again. He steps into the shower stall and slides the glass door shut. While he's standing there, he looks at something odd at the shower head.

For a moment he imagines a stream of gas coming from the nozzle instead of water. He does a double-take and then finds everything appears to be normal. He says out loud, ***"I must be more tired than I thought."***

He finishes his shower and towels off. Then he gets out his safety razor and shaving cream. By this time the water from the running shower has steamed up the medicine chest mirror. Paul wets his face, lathers up, and as he leans in close, he rubs the steam off the glass trying to see his reflection through the steamed up mirror.

Unable to see a clear image he reaches over and grabs a small hand towel to wipe the glass off. As he looks into the mirror, he sees a cloudy and distorted image of a cell door instead of his own reflection.

#2 –"Butcher"

Past the cell door he can make out the faint images of several people, all of them dressed alike. Each of them appears emancipated. His natural reflex is to reach out to prove to himself there is no cell door.

As he does, his hand passes into the mirror. Startled, he retracts it immediately. However, total curiosity drives him to reach back in a second time and as he does he grabs the cold steel of the cell door with his hand. As he touches the cell door he ends up rattling the steel door. A woman who is sitting on a bench across the cell looks up at him. She struggles to her feet and crosses the cell. Paul can see that she has a shaved head, and the expression on her face is less than friendly as she gets a good grip on the door with both of her hands, covering Paul's hand with her own, trapping it onto the bars of the cell door. He is started to feel her grasp on his hand.

Then she screams, ***"BOOTCHERRRRRR!"*** [Butcher]

She then spits into Paul's face. Paul reacts by yanking his hand free, and as he does he falls backwards until he ends up with his back against the opposite wall of his bathroom.

He reaches up and wipes the spit from his face then he watches the woman in the mirror smile. He glances down at his hand only to find shaving cream and not spit. He snaps his head up just in time to see her laughing image fade away into the steamy mist.

Paul is visibly shaken and cannot even speak. He shakes his head as if he could wake himself from this nightmare. Once assured he is back to normal he hastens to wipe off his face, and as he heads towards his bed, he thinks to himself. 'I've got to get some rest, that's all there's to it.' He takes some deep breaths and calls for Panda. Panda climbs up onto the bed, and soon the two of them are fast asleep.

Later, almost dawn

Paul is asleep. He has been tossing and turning, since the incident. But he has finally dozed off.

A woman enters the house, we see her legs only. She removes her shoes, dropping them at the foot of the stairs, then she quietly moves up, towards the master bedroom, one stair at a time. Paul is out cold.

We watch as her feet move closer and closer, up the stairway.

Panda lifts his head up, as he tries to listen. Then the woman enters the bedroom. Paul is out cold. But Panda's tail begins to wag. Walking to the opposite side of the bed she carefully sits on the mattress and she begins to disrobe. Paul wakes up a little bit startled.

Paul takes notice of her silhouette in the darkness, as she speaks***, "Sorry honey, I didn't mean to wake you."***

Paul recognizes Karen's voice, and he is reassured that it's only his wife, having just returned from her job. He rolls over, turning towards the opposite side of the bed, where he snaps on the lamp on his nightstand. While still turned away, he answers. ***"Yea, I guess I was having a bad dream."***

With the lamp on, he glances at his sleeping dog - Panda, and he turns to greet his wife. Much to his terror, he finds that it's the same woman he saw in the mirror. She doesn't speak but instead, stares at him with total hatred. Paul is paralyzed with fear and struggles to breathe.

Suddenly Paul's face telegraphs that he's fast asleep. His eyes are closed, he snaps them wide-open, then sits up into a prone position, as he does he screams. Panda is startled and he scrambles off the bed, headed downstairs.

Karen's bedroom lamp comes on, squinting from the harsh light, she leans towards Paul to comfort him. Paul jerks away, sweating and very shaken. She says, ***"Paul? It's me, Honey... try to relax sweetheart; you're having a bad dream, that's all."***

For a brief moment, Paul doesn't trust Karen's image. Then he silently nods, catching his breath and swallowing hard. He holds his chest as he struggles for a breath. When he finally regains his composure he says, ***"I'm alright now."***

Karen says, ***"Jesus Paul, you scared the shit out of me!"***

Paul's workplace

Paul arrives at work. He looks exhausted and pauses at the Receptionist's desk before entering his own office. He greets his receptionist, ***"Good morning, Barbara."***

Barbara replies, ***"Good Morning, Mr. Regis."***

Paul asks, ***"Any messages?"***

Barbara puts her reading glasses on and shuffles through some notes on her desk. Paul moves closer to his office door, and Barbara follows him into his office with her notes. Paul carefully hangs up his coat on a hall-tree, after setting his briefcase on the left side of his desk.

Barbara answers, ***"Uh, Baxter Motors called to remind you that your car is due for its semi-annual service, and, uh, speaking of appointments, you've got one with your Dentist at eight AM next Monday morning."***

Barbara pauses while she looks over her notes. ***"Oh eh, let's see... Mrs. Willoby called and mentioned that she spoke with her soon-to-be ex, and he apparently told her to shove any idea of a settlement up her..."***

Paul interrupts, ***"I specifically told her not to speak with her husband directly!"*** Paul looks irritated. Then he adds, ***"Barbara, get her on the line and set an appointment for Wednesday afternoon. Tell her that I'm very disappointed. Dammit! If I'm gonna be her***

attorney and offer some assistance, she has got to stop communicating with Roger, will you tell her that?"

Barbara nods and adds those instructions to her note pad. Paul gathers his thoughts. He asks, ***"Anything else?"***

Barbara adds, ***"Oh...uh, the Quigley boy's parents have made the decision to file suit. I set an appointment for next Thursday."***

Paul who has walked over to his office window to stare out at the impressive view from his office. He seems a little distant but musters up a small nod. Barbara pauses for a moment as if waiting for additional instructions.

She asks, ***"Shall I prepare the appeal documents for the Godard case, Mr. Regis?"***

Paul is in another world, as he continues staring out his window. Barbara clears her throat. This gets Paul's attention. Paul realizing that he's kept Barbara waiting, and he answers, ***"I'm sorry?"***

Barbara asks, ***"I was wondering if you wanted me to get started on the paperwork for the Godard appeal."***

Paul is obviously somewhat distracted. But he manages to answer, ***"Oh, uh, sure, that would be great, thanks Barbara."***

Barbara smiles and walks towards the office door. She stops and turns. ***"Coffee?"***

Paul is once again a million miles away. He doesn't answer. Barbara repeats her question, ***"Coffee, Mr. Regis?"***

Paul realizing that he's not quite in the moment answers, ***"I'm sorry Barbara, I was up late last night. Yea, coffee... that would be great!"***

Barbara leaves the room, closing the door softly behind her. Paul sits down at his desk, picks up a file folder and thumbs through it. There is a soft knock at his door.

He says, ***"Yes?"***

The door opens about a foot, a man in his early thirties pokes his head in Paul's office, looks at Paul and smiles. It's Larry Rector, one of the junior partners in the firm.

Larry notices Paul's smile and takes that as an invitation to enter and take a seat. He makes himself at home in one of the chairs directly in front of Paul's desk. Larry just sits there saying nothing and Paul is compelled to laugh, because Larry's such a character.

He asks, ***"What's up Larry?"***

Larry smiles and asks, ***"You'll never guess who I scored with last night!"***

Paul shuffles a few papers, filing them in a desk drawer, before answering, ***"I'm afraid to ask."***

Larry answers, ***"Veronica Hamlyn."***

Paul leans back in his chair shaking his head in a disapproving way. He looks at Larry with a frown. ***"I can't believe you, Larry!"***

Larry leans forward in his chair trying to explain, ***"Hey, relax. It's no big romance, Bro."***

Paul is obviously disappointed in his friend, ***"Is it ever? That's the problem Larry. "***

Larry looks away as if pondering Paul's criticism for all of a second. Then he smiles and makes a crude gesture with his two hands, mimicking Veronica breasts, before asking, ***"Guess what?"*** Paul gives him a look, and then shrugs his shoulders as if waiting for an explanation. Larry smiles and adds, ***"They're real."***

Paul looks at Larry in disbelief.

Larry raises his hand like a person on the witness stand, 'telling the truth, and nothing but the truth'. With that said, Larry adds, ***"I swear to God"***

Paul shakes his head in disbelief. Not at Larry's claims but at his chauvinistic attitude. He gets up from his desk and walks over to a filing cabinet. He opens the top drawer and then turns towards Larry. ***"Look, Larry..."*** He pauses. ***"I thought we've gone over this before?"*** He pulls a file from the cabinet and closes drawer. Then he sits down, before chastising Larry, like he has done so many times in the past. ***"Having personal relationships with clients is bad for***

business." He pauses. ***"Unless..."*** He pauses again.. ***"You're planning something serious, and permanent?"***

Larry looks at Paul in astonishment and points his thumb at himself. ***"Moi?"***

Paul snaps the file drawer closed and walks back to his desk with a file in hand. He's shaking his head at Larry in disbelief. ***"See? That's what I'm talking about! These casual encounters are going to be the death of you Larry!"*** He pauses. ***"Ultimately the firm will suffer too Larry. Remember when we were in college, planning to open up this office?"***

Larry nods. Then Paul continues, ***"No fooling around with the clients, right?"***

Larry flags Paul with his hand, ***"Yeah, yeah I know... I know."*** Larry pauses and stares at Paul with an 'I'm caught' look on his face. Then he tries to explain, ***"She was just trying to thank me for the superb job that I did for her on her divorce, that's all."***

Paul jumps right in to say, ***"She can do that by paying her fuckin' bill on time."***

Larry's silent and Paul gets a concerned look on his face. He asks, ***"She is gonna pay her bill, isn't she?"***

Larry perks up and smiles, then he taps his index finger on his temple before explaining, ***"I've got***

her ex-husband's attorney sending the settlement checks directly to us."

Paul laughs and shakes his head, wondering what he is going to do with Larry, like a parent wonders about a mischievous child. Larry gets up from the chair and moves towards the door with an air of confidence. He pauses at the door and looks back at Paul to add, ***"Besides, don't I always cover my ass?"***

Paul is forced to laugh in agreement, but mostly at Larry's antics. Then he tries to be funny by asking, ***"You sure they're real?"***

Larry smiles and starts to reenter the room to tell Paul all the sordid details about the night before, when Paul adds, ***"Will you get the hell out of here? Some of us have work to do."***

Larry backs out of the room with both hands raised. ***"OK, OK, I'm going, but you'll be sorry you didn't hear me out. And don't be begging me for information later? You had your chance!"***

A Fancy Lunch – Several days later

Paul, Larry, and an older more mature man are having lunch. The older man is the Senior Law Partner, Mr. Myron Crenshaw. Larry is just finishing up a joke as we come into their conversation.

Larry is laughing so hard he can hardly finish, ***"So, he asks her if she's missing anything, and he holds up a pair of woman's panties."***

The three men laugh, but Larry seems to be enjoying his own joke better than Myron and Paul. Myron becomes more serious and addresses Larry. ***"Look, Larry, about last night... "***

Larry interrupts Mr. Crenshaw by holding up his hands. ***"Myron, wait. Don't say it, I know. I fucked up."*** Larry glances at Paul for moral support. But Paul is obviously having a hard time with Larry's sincerity. Larry says, ***"I screwed up, OK? I'll try and be a little more discrete from now on."***

Paul smiles realizing that Larry might actually be serious. So, he lifts his glass to toast Larry's apology. He adds, ***"I propose a toast to Larry's new found celibacy, for however few minutes that it might last."***

All of them drink up and laugh the incident off, knowing full well that Larry has no intentions of ever changing. As the moment dies down, Myron looks at Paul in a serious manner. Myron says, ***"I'm a little worried about you too Paul."***

Paul smiles, looks at Larry first inquisitively and then back to Myron. ***"Me? For God's sake, why Myron?"***

Myron tries to explain, ***"Well, you've been looking a little ragged lately. Why don't you***

and that lovely wife of yours, take a few days off? Kind of a mini-vacation."

Paul starts to object by shaking his head. When Myron interrupts, ***"Now hear me out. I know you've been working your tail off on that Godard case. Larry tells me you've even been coming in on weekends, is that true?"***

Paul pleads his case***, "Only because Karen's been working some overtime at the hospital, I've just taken advantage of getting some extra work done, that's all."***

Myron doesn't believe a word of it. ***"Uh huh, just as I thought..."*** Myron smiles and pats Paul's shoulder. Then he adds***, "I'm sure Crenshaw, Regis, and Rector, can manage without you for a few days. Now I want you to take this weekend off, and relax a little bit, and I'm not taking no for an answer!"***

Paul looks a little concerned. He asks, ***"What about the Godard appeal? It has to be filed no later than Wednesday."***

Myron responds with a sense of urgency, ***"Oh for Christ's sake Paul. I'll put Larry on it, and I'm sure Barbara won't mind coming in a few hours early if need be, OK?"*** Paul smiles in approval at his senior partners plan. Then Myron says, ***"Besides..."*** He looks at Larry. ***"Despite "Valentino's" shortcomings, he's still a competent Attorney."***

Paul is skeptical, ***"Why do I get the feeling that the two of you are in cahoots?"***

Larry laughs at Paul's perceptive nature. Then he adds, ***"We are! Isn't that what friends are for?"***

There's a moment of silence as the three men sip their drinks. Then Myron speaks up, ***"Larry mentioned Karen and you, are going to some party tonight?"*** Paul nods yes. ***"Well then? Go! Have some fun and forget about work!"***

Larry chimes in, ***"Time to get your dancing shoes on bro, and boogie down!"***

Paul is always surprised by the comments that his wacky associate always comes up with. He comments. ***"Boogie down?"*** looking at Larry inquisitively, wondering where he picked up that expression. Larry shrugs his shoulders at both men and all three of them laugh together.

The Regis Bedroom

Karen's in bed after working most of the night before. The mood seems a little bit dark, and we're made to believe that something sinister might occur. Suddenly, the clock radio goes off. Karen reaches over sleepily and turns the volume down a bit. She stretches and gets out of bed yawning. She puts her robe on, and heads downstairs to the kitchen.

The Kitchen

It's a few minutes later and Karen is in the kitchen cooking herself some breakfast. The telephone breaks the silence. She crosses the room

Karen answers the phone, ***"Hello?"***

Paul's is at his desk, ***"Morning, Sleeping Beauty!"***

Karen laughs, ***"Oh hi, Baby."*** She walks back over to the stove, stretching the telephone cord across the room with her chin.

Paul explains the nature of his call, ***"Guess what? Myron thinks I've been working too hard around here. He wants me to take the whole weekend off."*** He pauses. ***"Want to drive up the coast and rent a motel?"***

Paul playfully changes his voice to that of a telephone masher. ***"We can get our nasty on."***

Karen laughs before saying, ***"What am I going to do with you... you pervert."***

Paul laughs and adds, ***"Take me into a dark room, and see what develops! What else?"***

Karen smiles at Paul's attempt to be funny, ***"Hey. By the way, don't forget to come straight home after work, OK? Remember, we're meeting Jerry and Michelle at seven at Rostina's."***

Paul asks, ***"Rostina's? Isn't that a little bit pricey for Jerry?"***

Karen laughs, ***"Oh, you know Jerry. He's still trying to impress Michelle."*** She pauses. ***"So, come right home, alright?"*** Karen waits a moment while Paul answers. Then she says, ***"Love you, Babe."*** She makes a kissy sound before saying, ***"Bye"*** then she hangs up the phone.

Paul at his desk

Paul hangs up the telephone, and silently ponders his wife Karen. He feels like a very lucky man to have her.

Gathering his business thoughts, he resumes working. As he begins to sort through Friday's mail, he automatically opens the top right-hand drawer of his desk, and without looking directly in it, he reaches for a letter opener but instead, withdraws a long silver dagger.

Unknowingly he brings it closer in order to open an envelope. That's when he spots the dagger, he's dumbfounded. Surprisingly it's not the letter opener that's usually in that drawer. He examines it, turning it over in his hand. On the handle he finds a Swastika. As he stares at it in amazement, Barbara knocks, opens his door, and steps into his office.

Paul does not acknowledge her entrance, but instead continues to stare at the mysterious dagger.

Barbara says, ***"I've got all of the paperwork started for the... "*** She stops mid-sentence as she notices Paul who is still staring at the dagger He hears her say something and looks up. He asks her, ***"Barbara, do you know who put this in my desk?"***

Paul holds out his right hand exposing a normal letter opener to Barbara. Barbara is a little confused at Paul's question, and answers it the only way she knows how. ***"I assume that you did, Mr. Regis."***

Paul gets an annoyed look on his face and continues to speak to her as he starts to turn his eyes towards his out-stretched palm. He begins to ask, ***"Barbara, this isn't..."***

That's when he notices that he's now holding a common letter opener, he becomes embarrassed at the tone of voice that he took with Barbara. He's suddenly flustered, ***"uh..."*** He pauses. ***"What I thought was, I uh... "*** He stops suddenly and says in an apologetic manner, ***"I eh, I guess maybe we had a few too many cocktails for lunch."***

Paul is lost for words and attempts a weak laugh. Barbara does her best to smile back before backing out of the room. We see her pause outside of Paul's office; she's concerned, regarding his behavior.

Regis kitchen later that evening

Karen is looking stunning in a new black dress that she recently bought for just an occasion such as tonight's rendezvous for dinner.

Paul just arrived from work and has not had a chance to get changed for tonight's event. He's sitting at their kitchen table and he is very animated as he explains the past two day's events to his wife over some wine and cheese.

He's very graphic as he stands up to demonstrate what happened, he pauses, looks at Karen who is listening intently. Paul finally wraps up his story of the day's events, and he re-takes his seat, putting a cracker in his mouth.

Karen asks, ***"And then what?"***

Paul answers, ***"Well..."*** He pauses before resuming his story, ***"I'm sure she thought I was the perfect idiot!"*** He pauses again. ***"Here I am, ready to jump all over her, I thought that Larry put her up to some joke? You know how he's always up to no good?"***

Karen nods in agreement. Then Paul adds, ***"Anyway, I played the part of a perfect ass."*** Karen, without thinking, nods yes and Paul stops in mid-sentence not at all amused that she agrees with his own assessment of his conduct.

Karen realizes her faux paux and tries to recover, ***"No, I don't mean that you're an ass... anyway, what happened after that?"***

Paul slumps in his chair, looking embarrassed. ***"Nothing! She just gave me that... 'I think he's finally flipped out' look! Then she smiled politely and left the room."***

Karen begins to laugh. She covers her mouth with her hand to hide her reaction. Paul is not amused in the slightest by his wife's reaction. He asks, ***"Karen. I fail to see the humor in this! I'm probably going crazy, and now my wife is laughing her butt off at me!"***

Karen regrets her reaction and moves closer to hug her husband. ***"I'm sorry sweetheart; I know it's not funny. But I don't think it's too serious to get all worked up about either. I see this kind of thing all the time at the hospital. It's probably just a little stress, that's all."***

Paul finally smiles and +offers Karen a reassuring nod. Then he seems to perk right up, ***"Come on, let's get ready to go... we'll have a little fun tonight, ok?"***

She kisses him on the lips. And then adds sarcastically, ***"I've been ready for more than an hour sweetie, so get a move on."***

Rostina's Restaurant

We see Paul and Karen arrive at the restaurant.

In the lobby the Maître d' begins to check reservations for Jerry Spaulding's name;

meanwhile, Paul and Karen scan the room looking for Jerry. They spot him, he's waving from a booth in the rear of the dining room.

They excuse themselves from the Maître d', making their way on their own, across the floor of the restaurant. There sits Jerry Spaulding and his girlfriend, Michelle.

Jerry shakes Paul's hand as Paul and Karen take their seats. He speaks up, ***"Hi kids... you know Michelle?"*** Michelle smiles and greets the two of them. Karen addresses Michelle, ***"Well Michelle, I can see that you're managing to survive, hanging out with Jerry."***

Jerry interrupts, ***"Hey, I've changed! She actually likes me Karen. It's possible, you know?"***

Karen smacks her lips, and laughs. Shaking her head in disbelief. She looks at Jerry and says, ***"Yeah? I'll believe it when I see it!"***

Jerry lets out a sardonic laugh. Then he adds, ***"I'm worse now. So, you need to give Michelle some credit."***

The group laughs. Jerry looks at Paul. ***"So how goes it, Paul?"***

Paul smiles and adds, ***"Same old shit, different day. You know."***

Michelle chimes in, ***"I bet your work is interesting though, have you defended any famous criminals?"***

Paul chuckles, wondering what kind of stories Jerry's told her about him. He answers, ***"Criminals? Criminals don't have money. Our firm handles industrial lawsuits, corporate mergers, and run of the mill divorce cases. Mundane stuff like that, nothing spectacular."***

Jerry looks at Michelle and adds, ***"Paul's really bored with his work... "*** He looks at Paul and smiles. ***"All the way to the bank, eh buddy?"***

Paul smiles confidently back at Jerry and shrugs the comment off. Then he asks, ***"So, what about you? You're not doing too bad, or so it seems?"***

Jerry rolls his head to the right, and shrugs his shoulders, ***"Eh?"***

Paul responds, ***"Rostina's?"*** Jerry smiles smugly, then Paul jokes with him, ***"What'd you do, put on a set of extra braces this week?"***

Jerry (putting on an act) answers, ***"You know how tough life is, being a dentist? You ask people for their opinions and all they do is grunt***!" He pauses. ***"It's a lonely profession."***

Jerry gestures. ***"You do a load of fillings here, a few extractions there, some unnecessary x-rays, and a couple of root canals for good measure, and... voila' suddenly you have a three story home in the Hamptons."***

Jerry laughs at himself, hoping the rest of them know he's only kidding. Then he adds, ***"Shit Paul, what's the big deal? We're all milking the system in our own little way, right?"***

Paul is holding up his head with one hand, and he sighs at Jerry's honesty. ***"Uh, huh."***

The mood is broken by the arrival of the cocktail waitress.

She asks, ***"Can I get any of you something to drink?"***

Karen responds first. ***"I'll have a Pina' Colada, and directions to the Little Girls Room."***

The waitress points in the proper direction. That's when Karen speaks to Michelle, ***"Come with me, girlfriend. You can tell me all about the way Jerry's been mistreating you."***

As the two women slide out of the booth, Michelle leans over before walking away to join Karen. She whispers to Jerry that she'd like a white wine.

Jerry speaks to the waitress, ***"A white wine for the lady, and I'll have some peppermint schnapps over."***

The waitress leans closer to Paul, ***"And what can I get you sir?"***

Paul smiles and says, ***"I think I'll have a Strawberry Daiquiri."***

The waitress adds, ***"OK. Coming right up."*** And she walks away.

Jerry explains, ***"I guess it's an old habit, but I always get Peppermint Schnapps. That way, when I have a liquid lunch my patients don't know that I've had a few drinks."***

Paul tries to joke with Jerry, ***"Until they get home and discover that you pulled the wrong tooth."*** Now that the two men are by themselves, Paul asks, ***"So, how are things going between you and Michelle?"***

Jerry laughs before answering, and then he leans over closer to Paul and says something in German. Then he smiles as if waiting for an answer.

Paul frowns because he did not understand a word out of Jerry's mouth. He asks, ***"Did you just speak German to me?"***

Jerry shrugs his shoulders and smiles, ***"German?"*** He looks at Paul perplexed. Then he tries to make a joke, ***"Whatever kind of drugs you're taking... spread the joy around, would ya?"***

Paul has to laugh at Jerry's suggestive question, and he answers, ***"Who's got time for drugs?"*** Both men are smiling but remain silent. Then Paul suddenly says, ***"But I have had time for some weird nightmares that I could do without."*** He pauses briefly. Then he asks himself, ***"Working too hard, I guess. At least that's what the senior partner at our law firm thinks. So, Karen and I are going to take a little time off."***

The restaurant's cocktail waitress returns with the drinks. The waitress' lifts Paul's glass from her serving tray, and she sets it down on a small end table at a completely different location. Suddenly we are transported to the cocktail party.

During this transition the background sounds of the party increase, making us more and more aware that a change has occurred.

Paul is sitting on one side of a little end-table, he looks up to thank the cocktail waitress for the drink, but she seemed to have vanished. Then a beautiful woman who is facing Paul, on the same couch asks, ***"And what does your wife Karen do?"***

Paul is still bewildered that the cocktail waitress has seemed to disappear. Then he hears the voice of the woman who is sitting at the other end of the couch. He tries to answer as if he hasn't missed a beat, ***"As I was saying..."*** His eyes shift from the woman to where the cocktail waitress was just standing, and then back to the woman. ***"...she's an R.N., over at St. Marks Hospital."***

Paul looks up at all the other guests before finally seeing Jerry who is waving his arm trying to get Paul's attention. He motions that Paul should come over and join him. Paul smiles and then looks back at the woman he was speaking with. ***"Would you please excuse me for a moment?"***

She smiles and Paul gets up, crossing the room to where Jerry is standing. He notices right away that Jerry is a little tipsy. Jerry says, ***"Hey, you've got to come in the kitchen with me."***

Paul asks, ***"What's up?"***

Jerry let's out a demonic laugh. Then he commands, ***"Just follow me... There's an old bitch in there, reading palms."***

Paul stops short and Jerry comes to a full stop at the end of Paul's sleeve. Paul gives Jerry his excuse for not wanting to see a fortune teller.

Paul explains, ***"Uh, look Jerry, I really don't believe in that shit."***

Jerry laughs and slaps Paul on the shoulder. He says, ***"Other than Shirley Maclaine, who in the fuck does? But you've got to get a load of this old croaker non-the-less."***

Paul thinks about resisting Jerry's tugging for a moment, and then he reluctantly follows.

Jerry adds, ***"Come on, it's "painless!"***

Paul reluctantly follows and as he does he tells Jerry, ***"I'm not one of your patients, Jerry."***

As they reach the swinging kitchen door, Jerry stops to add some words of wisdom. He laughs and says, ***"Look at it this way. Maybe she'll be able to shed some light on those nightmares you've been having?"*** The two men enter the kitchen together.

#3 – "Route to Seance"

The Kitchen

The kitchen is dark and only illuminated by a single candle on the table. Several people are crowded around it, paying close attention to an old woman who has the palm of another woman in her own hands.

Jerry drags Paul into the room with no regard for the noise they are making. Several people in the group "shush" them. Jerry looks at Paul and tries unsuccessfully to muffle a laugh, then moves his index finger to his lips in mockery of the imposed silence.

Paul seems to become more and more interested in what the old woman has to say, than Jerry's antics.

The Fortune Teller faces the woman across the table from her, but she speaks out to the room, ***"You have a gift."*** She pauses. Then she says, ***"You're a 'healer', yes? Maybe a Doctor? No, no, a Nurse. Yes, that's it! You're a Nurse!"***

For the first time we realize that the old woman has been speaking to Paul's wife, Karen. Karen smiles at the woman's comment. She says, ***"That's right, I am!"***

The woman leans back confidently as the small group politely claps. They all seem quite astonished. The old woman looks around at the others. She asks, ***"Who will be next for a journey into the past, the present, or the future?"***

Jerry pulls Paul trying to persuade him to participate. Paul pulls his arm back from Jerry's grasp, as he physically resists. Jerry says, ***"Come on, you turkey. Go for it!"***

Everyone in the quiet kitchen shushes Jerry. Karen hears Jerry's voice and looks up spotting Paul in the group. Seeing Paul, she perks right up and says, ***"Come on, Honey. Give it a try."*** The rest of the guests encourage Paul.

Paul addresses the group, ***"I'm sorry everyone, but I just don't believe in this sort of thing, I'm sorry."***

The Fortune Teller interrupts Paul, ***"Your belief is not required to participate."***

Jerry nudges Paul once again, ***"Go on, buddy."***

Finally, Paul nods reluctantly, that he'll participate. ***"Oh, all right, geez. But it won't change my mind!"***

Karen stands up and Paul takes her seat at the kitchen table. directly across from the old woman. She stares into his eyes.

The Fortune Teller responds, ***"It's not designed to 'change' your mind. But if we're lucky, maybe we can open it a little bit, huh?"***

Paul let's off a small sarcastic chuckle as the old woman takes his hand and examines his palm closely***. "Oh! I can see right away that you're a professional man."***

Paul is obviously astonished! He asks, ***"You saw that in my palm?"***

The old woman looks dead serious into Paul's eyes, and in a somewhat sarcastic manner she says, ***"One just has to take a look at hands like these to see that they haven't done any, "real work," in a very, very, long time!"***

Everyone in the room laughs at the woman's quick wit and her ability to put Paul in his place. Paul smiles, even he can appreciate her sense of humor. She gets more serious studying his palm even closer. She says, ***"I can see that you are a very sensitive person, a loving person."***

She pauses.

"You're also very lucky to have reunited with your soul mate from a previous lifetime. You were very much in love as you are presently."

Paul realizes that although he may not believe in most of this, he had to agree that Karen is very special to him. He musters up a small grin. He asks, ***"Tell me more about that previous life?"***

The Fortune Teller answers, ***"That's a cloudy period. Another more recent life, perhaps***

your current life, blocks the path. The old life is struggling to take over the new life. It's also making things difficult for me to distinguish between the two."

She pauses.

"However, I can see that you're what we call a 'mature soul'. You're an artesian on the fifth level of life, with interests in self-growth and spiritual awareness. This is your last life here on Earth and you're hungry for knowledge. The intellectual part of your emotional center is the source of this ambition. In this stage, your soul is impatient."

Paul being curious asks, ***"What do you mean by 'this stage'?"***

She takes a long look into Paul's eyes, knowing full well that he will be reluctant to accept her explanation. She continues, regardless. ***"You see, many people including me, believe that we have all lived before, in other times, as other people."*** She pauses and Paul nods. Then she continues, ***"We've had other bodies, different personalities. Do you understand?"***

Speaking before Paul can answer, ***"I do not expect you to believe any of this. I merely serve as the vehicle. Think of me as an instrument, a tool, a way to get answers to your questions."***

Paul being curious asks, ***"What questions?"***

The Fortune Teller answers, ***"Your soul is troubled right now. You want answers, and that other energy source is very strong right now."***

Paul asks, ***"What energy source? I don't quite understand."***

The Fortune Teller says, ***"The energy source connected with this troubled life... lies somewhere in your past..."*** She pauses, then she continues, ***"It's clear to me, that you've attained self-satisfaction in this 'present' life. Today's challenges no longer cloud your sub-conscious. You're thinking clearly now, and you're open to inner forces. The sub-conscious is calling out, trying to communicate, trying to answer questions you may not even know to ask."***

She leans in and looks deeper into Paul's eyes. ***"I'm afraid I can't tell you more. You're not ready to let go so the answers can come forward."***

Paul looks at The Fortune Teller as if he was cheated and yanks his hand away. Sarcastically he shouts, "That's absurd!"

The room is silent at Paul's reaction. Paul stares into the Fortune Teller's eyes for a moment then he smiles, adding, ***"But still entertaining, nonetheless."***

The tension seems to be reduced. Just then the kitchen door bursts open, and a drunken woman pokes her head into the dark kitchen and yells. ***"Is my Harry in there? Harry?"***

The woman pops the kitchen light on and breaks the entire mood. The people in the room are disappointed but realize it's late and the group begins to break up.

As they disperse, Jerry moves closer to Paul and Karen, whistling music like we've all heard at Horror Movies. Obviously mocking the whole ordeal. He laughs out loud as he attempts to speak to Paul. ***"So-ooo, the old bag sez you've got a troubled life huh? She should see your portfolio!"***

Karen embarrassed at Jerry's loud comment about the woman comes to her rescue***, "Jerry, for God's sake!"***

Jerry puts his index-finger to his lips and laughs, then he waves towards the kitchen door. ***"Eh she didn't hear me, she's half way home on her broom by now."*** He turns towards Paul. ***"Well... what'd you think?"***

Paul sits silent looking at the kitchen door where the woman inside may have changed his life. When he realizes that Jerry has said something he says, ***"Huh ?"***

Jerry repeats what he said, ***"The old geezer's predictions?"***

Paul pauses and looks at Jerry with a blank stare, he doesn't answer, but just walks away. Paul stands up with a sense of urgency, starts making his way out of the kitchen ignoring Jerry altogether. Under the weather and now a little pissed, Jerry turns towards Karen.

Jerry looks at Karen and asks, ***"You making sure your old man is gettin' enough protein?"***

Karen smiles and takes Jerry's drink away from him. She points him at the coffee pot. Then she adds, ***"Come on Jerr', if you're gonna take that nice lady of yours home safely, you'd better get some coffee into those veins."***

In the entrance area of this home. Several people are congregating because it's getting late. They're retrieving their coats for the trip home. The old woman has retrieved her coat, scarf, hat, and gloves. Paul sees her from across the room and makes his way to her side.

Pail speaks, ***"Excuse me?"*** He feels awkward, but he asks anyway, ***"I, uh, I'm sorry if I sounded a little pessimistic in there."***

The woman wraps her scarf around her neck. Puts on her beret and then turns to search Paul's eyes for a little sincerity. She smiles gently, cupping his hand between her two gloved hands. She says, ***"Many people resist at first."*** She takes a moment to pause, then she smiles and begins walking towards the front door.

Paul speaks up, ***"I suppose that should be expected, huh?"***

She stops and turns to look him in the eyes. Then she says, ***"Some people should come to terms with their past."*** She starts heading for the front door, and then turns back to Paul... flagging him over with her hand. ***"You must be willing to accept the good with the bad. Both, always accompany knowledge such as this. Nothing comes without a price. Can you accept that, Mister, uh?"***

She pauses, holding out her hand in friendship. PAUL lifts his hand to meet hers as he introduces himself, ***"Regis. Paul Regis."***

She responds by saying, ***"You have a nice wife, Mr. Regis".*** She smiles. ***"And you're not so bad yourself. I hope you find the answers that you're looking for?"***

She smiles and leaves the house. As she reaches the walkway Paul rushes outside to ask her one last question, he reaches out and touches her shoulder. She turns.

Paul asks her, ***"Could you recommend someone that might be able to help me?"***

She pauses to think. Then she answers, ***"I have an acquaintance that I've worked with a few times. A doctor."*** She pauses. ***"Dr. Michael Shay. Yes, if I were you Mr. Regis, I'd contact Dr. Shay. He's a hypnotherapist, and***

he's done some research in the area of Past Life Regression. I think you'd gain a lot from the experience." She pauses. ***"Providing of course..."*** Paul looks up. ***"That you keep an open mind."***

Paul smiles at her subliminal message, and then he asks, ***"How can I reach him?"***

The Fortune Teller answers, ***"Don't you or your wife have one of those smart phones? Don't worry, you'll find him. Dr. Michael Shay."*** A car pulls up and she gets inside the backseat. She rolls down the window and says, ***"Goodnight Mr. Regis. I wish you all my best."***

Later that same night

Paul and Karen are getting ready for bed. Paul is hanging his clothes up in the closet, Karen is in the bathroom picking her face in the mirror.

Karen says, ***"Man. Jerry's gonna have a headache tomorrow."***

Paul comments, ***"Yea? I noticed he was tying one on early. I hope he didn't try to drive home?"***

Karen answers, ***"I tried feeding him some coffee earlier tonight; but he was already too far gone, Michelle took away his car keys and told me that she'd be driving him home."***

She walks from the bathroom, crosses the room, and sits in front of the vanity where she begins to brush her hair.

Karen says, ***"I think I'm gonna go downstairs and fix myself some hot chocolate, want some?"***

Paul holds one hand up and clutches his stomach with the other. He shakes his head 'no'. Karen tries again, ***"It might make you sleep a little better?"***

Paul finally insists, ***"No thanks. I feel marginally OK now, but I don't think I should push it."***

Karen smiles, lays her brush down, walks over to where Paul is standing, gently hugs him and kisses his cheek.

Karen says, ***"I want to thank you for putting up with Jerry and Michelle***." She pauses and then asks, ***"The Fortune Teller said that you're very much in love with me. Is that true?"***

Paul smiles and asks, ***"What do you think?"***

It's a very tender moment of silence as Karen's smile is traded for a serious intense stare. She slowly moves closer to Paul's face and they kiss passionately. Karen's robe falls to the floor.

The Kitchen – The Next Morning

Karen is preparing breakfast, Paul in a sleep induced stupor stumbles in. He walks over to her, gives her a hug, laying his head on her shoulder mimicking a snore.

Karen laughs, sets the cooking utensils down, escorts him over to the table and sits him down. The table is already set for breakfast.

Karen speaks to him, ***"Here ya go. Today's newspaper."*** She picks up the electric coffee pot off the table and pours him a cup of coffee... adding, ***"and a nice hot cup of fresh brewed coffee."*** She pauses. ***"Bacon and eggs on the way."***

Paul smiles and asks, ***"Why all the service?"***

Karen answers, ***"Oh... just because."***

Karen gives Paul a long sexy stare, then she walks back towards the sink. She speaks as she moves. ***"Larry called early this morning."***

Paul responds, ***"I didn't hear the phone ring."***

Karen brings a plate of food and sets it in front of Paul. She playfully laughs, ***"That's because you were still sawing logs, silly."***

Paul smiles and begins to eat his meal. He takes a couple of gulps of his coffee, and when he sets his mug on the table, Karen immediately refills his cup. She sets the pot back down and takes a seat. Then she continues, ***"Besides, I told him you were out."***

Paul frowns at her white lie. Karen responds to Paul's disapproval, ***"Well, you "were, out" in a manner of speaking... so I wasn't lying!"***

Paul raises one eyebrow and smiles. He asks, ***"Did he say what he wanted?"***

Karen shakes her head, ***"No, just heavy breathing!"*** She smirks. ***"I'm kidding. Of course. He wanted to know where the documents were, that Barbara started? For the Guttard case?"***

Paul asks, ***"You mean Godard?"***

Karen a little bit annoyed, ***"Guttard, Godard, whatever. I asked him if Barbara was scheduled to come in and he said 'Oh, yea, sorry, and he hung up. It seemed like a major revelation that he could have simply contacted Barbara to begin with"***. She pauses and then asks, ***"Does he do anything around there on his own?"***

Paul seems a bit concerned and suggests, ***"You should have probably woke me."***

Karen does not reply and instead finishes her own breakfast, then she arranges the silverware on her empty plate and walks it to the sink. She explains, ***"Oh... and Larry said that Myron told him that, he wanted you to take the whole weekend off including Monday and Tuesday;***

and that's the way I'd like to keep it, seeing as I've already made all the arrangements for someone to cover me while I'm out."

She turns to Paul and then adds, ***"Besides, you were the one that suggested a trip up the coast this weekend, remember? If we had already left as planned, no one would have been here to answer Larry's phone call anyway. But as luck would have it, we ended up with a couple of extra days off."***

Paul lifts his coffee cup to toast her, he smiles. Karen walks back to the table, takes her seat, and reaches out and lifts Paul's hand. ***"So... Let's get going!"***

Paul smiles at his wife's enthusiasm, ***"Up the coast? Now?"***

Karen is obviously excited, as she says, ***"Yes. Right now. Let's just be spontaneous!"***

Paul asks, ***"But we don't have any reservations."***

Karen instantly responds, ***"So what? We'll come home if we can't find a place to stay. You remember me talking about Kathy, from work? The gal in pediatrics?"*** Paul nods. ***"She suggested that we'd enjoy ourselves more if we found one of those little Bed and Breakfast Inns. They're more romantic than a Motel."***

Paul is becoming quite excited at his wife's enthusiasm, ***"OK. But let's pack a few things in case we get lucky and find a B&B."***

Karen coyly smiles, ***"Already done!"***

Paul is surprised, ***"Done?"***

Karen smiles and takes his empty coffee cup to the sink. While standing at the couple's sink she turns to address Paul, ***"While you were gettin' your beauty rest, I packed a couple of overnight bags."***

Paul smiles, and trying to be the consummate comedian asks, ***"Did you remember to pack our 'sex-toys'?"***

Karen stops talking abruptly, and she stares at Paul in disbelief before asking, ***"We have sex toys?"***

Paul laughs at his wife's gullible response. That's when Karen realizes that Paul is trying to be funny. She claps her hands, and says, ***"Sooo? Chop, chop! Get a move on, slowpoke!"*** And she turns to rinse the breakfast dishes.

Paul stretches and yawns. ***"OK but give me a few minutes to shower."***

#4 – "Trepidation"

Regis' Master Bedroom

Paul steps into their bathroom, he closes the door, and walks over to the shower stall, where he reaches in and turns on the water. Then he drops his robe to the floor. His naked feet find their way into the shower. He turns the water on and adjusts the pressure. His hand slides the glass shower door closed behind himself, as he steps into the stream.

He lathes up his hair, his face, and his chest. Then he hears something unusual. This causes him to stop as he tries to identify the sound. He hastily rinses the soap from his eyes, as he takes a look around in the small shower stall. He shakes his head, smiles at his own imagination, and begins to wash himself off in the stream of water. Suddenly the water stops, and he looks up at the nozzle.

Paul is mortified. He's suddenly worried that he won't have any water to completely rinse off, and he thinks that something must have gone wrong with the plumbing. He speaks out loud, ***"What the fuck?"***

He fiddles with the nozzle, twisting the faucets and banging his fist on the wall below the shower head to no avail. Thinking that Karen might know something about this, he calls out her name knowing full well that she probably won't be able to hear him anyway. ***"Karen? Karen honey?"***

He finds that his voice is echoing as if he's in a huge room instead of their tiny shower stall. For a second he becomes a little frightened and spirals around only to find himself in a room approximately twenty by twenty.

Two-dozen or more naked people are standing in there with him. Paul is startled and gasps for air at this sight, he turns to escape through the shower stall door. Instead of the door he finds a solid brick wall. He realizes that he's trapped!

He slowly turns back towards the others, dripping wet. The others seem oblivious to him, they are also frightened. A second later a small hissing sound begins. People begin panicking and they start looking around the room trying to find some way out.

That's when Paul notices gas coming from several of the other showerheads, he turns and is horrified that it's also coming from his own.

In a panic he tries unsuccessfully to hold back the stifling gas with his bare hand. He begins to cough violently, he's frantic now... calling for Karen. ***"Karen!"*** He screams hysterically. ***"Karen, help me!"***

With his hand grasping the shower head Paul begins to pass out and he drops to the floor, as the gas overcomes him.

As it turns out Karen did hear his cries for help, and she's frantically trying to get the bathroom door open. Her first thought is how unusual it is that her husband would even lock the bathroom door in the first place. She tries to answer her husband's cries through the door, and then she finally starts slamming her shoulder into it to gain entry. The door finally gives way, swinging open. As it does, Paul falls out of the shower stall and onto the bathroom floor unconscious. Karen puts her hand to her mouth, and screams!

The Master Bedroom.

A Doctor gently closes the bedroom door behind himself. He pauses for a moment, looking back towards the room then makes his way down the stairs. He enters the living room where Karen is waiting patiently. He sits down. The moment that she sees him, she immediately looks very concerned.

The Doctor speaks up***, "He's resting comfortably now."***

Karen immediately asks, ***"Is he going to be all right?"***

The Doctor smiles to put Karen's mind at ease. He adds, ***"He'll be just fine. I gave him a little something that'll calm him down a bit. I think that he'll be just fine in a couple of hours."*** He pauses. ***"I'll say one thing for him. He certainly has a vivid imagination."*** The doctor inquires, ***"Can he arrange for a few days off from his job?"***

Karen answers as a medical person herself, ***"You can count on it, Doctor."***

The Doctor smiles, ***"Good, good."*** And he stands as he gets ready to leave. Karen feels compelled to tell him about their little get away, ***"In fact, we were getting ready to go up the coast when this happened."***

The Doctor smiles, adding, ***"Well... I don't see any reason why you should change your plans. A trip like that is better medicine than any pill that I could give him."***

The Doctor excuses himself and heads towards the front door. At the front door he stops to address Karen. ***"He'll be just fine, I'm sure of it."*** Then he adds, ***"Now don't worry. He's just been burning the midnight oil too much, that's all. Stress like that catches up with the best of us. Your trip will be the best medicine."***

Karen smiles in agreement, then she thanks the doctor for coming, ***"Thank you, Doctor."***

Karen sees him out, and then walks to the foot of the stairs with a worried look on her face. She pauses, shakes it off, gets a smile on her face (attempting to change her attitude) and ascends the stairway.

#5 - "The Journey"

Driving up the coast later that day

Karen and Paul are finally on their way up the coast. Karen is at the wheel; Paul is sitting on the passenger side looking out the window. He has his index finger across his lips as if he's deep in thought. He turns towards Karen and speaks. It's obvious that this is one of the first words that he's said for many hours.

Paul asks, ***"So? What did that doctor have to say? Am I losing my mind?"***

Karen bursts out with a laugh, then covers her mouth and looks at Paul sympathetically. ***"I'm sorry, Honey."*** She pauses. ***"It's really not that serious. The Doctor said you've been working too hard, that's all. These things happen when the body's under a lot of stress."***

Paul looks a bit down and answers, ***"Sounds like a scene from and old movie."*** Karen stifles a laugh. Then Paul continues, ***"Hummm... Working too hard, huh?"***

Karen glances at Paul in a sympathetic manner. She reaches over and places her hand on his knee. She tries to be supportive, ***"Come on... let's not worry about it anymore, OK? Were on a holiday. If we're gonna worry, let's worry about getting a reservation."*** Paul looks at her, smiles and nods in approval. Then she adds, ***"Besides, your worries are over!"*** She pauses as Paul looks on inquisitively. Then she adds, ***"Larry Rector is in charge while were gone!"***

Paul frowns at her sarcasm. He doesn't consider Larry to be the best choice to run a law practice by himself, and he says, ***"Great! That's what I needed to hear. That isn't doing much to put my mind at ease."***

The two of them enjoy a much-needed laugh, the tension of Paul's problem seems to leave them both for the moment.

Paul asks, ***"What happened with you and the hospital, you never said?"***

Karen smiles and explains, ***"Nothing really. I have so many hours sandbagged that there was no problem getting the time off."*** She pauses. ***"I simply told them that I needed a few days. Besides, I've got almost nine weeks of vacation time saved up. They can certainly spare me for a few days."***

She pauses and then looks at Paul like a kid planning some mischief. ***"By the way, Kathy from work called yesterday with a recommended place to stay. With all the excitement I forgot to call them. Hopefully when we arrive, they'll have a vacancy."***

She pauses and looks at Paul playfully, ***"Think you can handle me for the next couple of days?"***

Paul smiles and slides over on the seat next to her. He places his arm around her shoulders and tries to kiss her on the neck. Paul laughs, ***"I'd start handling you now, if you weren't driving."***

Karen smiles and glances at him in a sexy way, before adding, ***"That never stopped you before."***

Over the next few days, we see the two of them enjoying themselves. Paul is driving now, and he seems to be renewed.

They sign up for horseback rides, and both of them are seen snapping a lot of pictures with their phones. It's late in the afternoon and they're headed back to the motel, Karen is leaning against her husband. She asks, ***"Paul?"***

Paul answers, ***"Yea?"***

Karen seems happy and she says, ***"I'm really glad we came. I'd almost forgotten how much fun you are."***

Paul smiles at her. ***"Me to!"***

Karen asks, ***"How you feeling?"***

Paul ponders her question, his mental, as well as physical state before answering, ***"Good!"*** He pauses. ***"No. Actually, I feel great!"*** He looks at her. ***"I do! I feel like this trip was long overdue. Now, let's hope Larry didn't screw up the entire office."***

Lobby of Paul's workplace

Paul enters the office for the first time since he left. He's greeted by Barbara (the receptionist).

"Good morning, Mr. Regis. How was your vacation?"

Paul knows by her comment that Barbara knows nothing about his little problem. He moves towards his office, coat, and briefcase in hand, as he responds. ***"Absolutely fantastic Barbara! Thanks for asking. Is Larry in yet?"***

Barbara stands and follows Paul into his office before answering. ***"Yes, he is, shall I ask him to come to see you?"***

Paul takes his seat as he gets settled in. ***"No, uh, I'll catch up with him later. Well..."*** He pauses, looking around his desk and office, getting reacquainted with his surroundings. Then he asks, ***"Did I miss much?"***

Barbara diligently responds, ***"Well, not really things sort of slowed down. Mr. Rector and I processed all the necessary documents for the Godard appeal on Saturday and I filed them with the clerk's office on Monday morning. Everything went rather well with that."*** She interrupts herself and looks at Paul. ***"We were issued a court date for Mid-June, which should allow considerable time to prepare the agenda."*** She looks down at her notes. ***"I, uh, oh..."*** She pauses. ***"I rescheduled your dental appointment for next Wednesday afternoon. And, uh, the Quigley's are set to come in this afternoon at three thirty."***

Paul looks up. ***"They'll be wanting to discuss their son's injury case."***

Then Barbara adds, ***"Also, Mr. Crenshaw called, he wants you to try to reach him at the Ambassador Hotel in Denver."***

Paul is surprised and asks, ***"Denver? What's he doing in Denver?"***

Barbara explains, ***"The Hudson Ski Corporation called on Friday after you left and requested our assistance with two civil injury cases filed against the company. I guess he decided to help out while you were gone."***

Paul asks, ***"I wonder why they didn't just call a local attorney?"***

Barbara tries to clarify things, ***"Well, from what I gathered, Mr. Crenshaw went to college with Stacy Hudson, the owner? I'm sure that influenced his decision to help."***

Paul laughs to himself, shakes his head and mumbles under his breath. ***"So much for mixing with the clients."***

Barbra didn't quite hear Paul, and asks, ***"Pardon?"***

Paul smiles and responds, ***"Oh, uh, nothing."***

The moment is broken by Larry Rector's arrival in Paul's office. Larry chimes in, ***"Well. Hello stranger. Hope you had a good time while the rest of us were busy at work?"***

Paul smiles and flags Larry into his office with his hand. ***"Come on in, Larry."***

Barbara leaves the room, closing the door behind her. Larry moves over to one of the two arm chairs in front of Paul's desk. He sits down swinging one leg up on the arm of the chair. Then he pulls out a fingernail file from his breast pocket and starts to primp himself before speaking, ***"I guess Barbara told you all about Myron? Imagine that. The old fart rushes off to Denver to see his old flame. Could this be a case of 'do as I say', and not, 'do as I do'?"***

Paul tries to defend the boss, ***"I think this is a little different Larry. Myron met Stacy Hudson in college a long, long, time ago."***

Larry waves his hand as if he really doesn't give a shit, before letting Paul hear his words of wisdom, ***"It really doesn't bother me. Even the old man needs "a little pussy", once in a while, right?"***

Paul reluctantly smirks at Larry's humor. Then Larry changes the subject. ***"So, tell me. How was your trip?"***

Paul leans back in his chair, places his hands behind his head and smiles. ***"Man, I can't begin to tell you how great it was."*** He pauses and then leans forward. ***"But I'm glad to be back. You know how it is, 'no place like home'."***

Larry smiles, ***"You mean, 'no place like someone else's home', as in 'your place or mine'?"***

Paul shakes his head at Larry's attempt to be funny. Larry stands and walks towards the door. He turns and says, ***"I'll get the Godard paperwork from Barbara. I'm sure your anxious to see what a great job I did."***

With Paul still smiling, Larry closes the door behind himself. Paul reaches over and switches on the intercom. ***"Barbara?"***

Barbara answers, ***"Yes Mr. Regis?"***

Paul asks, ***"Would you do me a favor and see if you can find the telephone number for a Doctor Michael Shay? He should be listed under Physicians, and if not... try Hypnotherapy. By the way, just a heads up... here comes trouble."***

Barbara asks, ***"Sir?"***

Paul answers, ***"Larry."***

Dr. Michael Shay's Office

Paul is attending an appointment at Doctor Shay's office. He is busy describing the vivid hallucinations that he's been experiencing over the past few weeks. His experiences seem very vivid as he explains, ***"The next thing I knew, I'm waking up on the floor, in Karen's arms. I was a basket case, scared to death!"*** The

Doctor is listening intently. Paul continues, ***"I mean, the whole incident was so real. Just like I was there!"***

Doctor Shay says, ***"Maybe you were?"***

Paul shakes his head a bit confused, ***"I don't understand?"***

Doctor Shay smiles and leans closer to Paul before trying to explain, ***"Often a person will experience a 'window'. An opening if you will. A clear channel to an experience that may have occurred in the past. Possibly even their own past."***

Paul is still trying to digest everything that Dr. Shay is describing. Doctor Shay can sense his struggle and continues to do his best to clarify things for Paul. ***"You see, there are theories that exist, which adhere to the belief that each of us has lived full lives on Earth, before."*** Doctor Shay pauses. ***"If those theories are correct, each of us may have lived hundreds of times, with past lives dating back to the beginnings of man."***

Doctor Shay pauses again. ***"I feel that your experiences and the subsequent stress, is what Clara felt. And ultimately why she suggested you contact me."***

Paul interrupts, ***"Clara ? You mean the Fortune Teller I met at the party?"***

Doctor Shay answers, ***"Yes. Clara Nelson. Oh, I'm sorry, I thought you two were properly introduced?"***

Paul sheepishly smiles, ***"Actually, I'm not sure that I caught her name. Things happened so fast that night, before I knew it she was gone."***

Doctor Shay smiles, ***"Well... ?"***

He pauses and then adds, ***"Clara Nelson was a student of mine. I taught a short class last summer at Pepperdine College on 'The Medical Interpretation of Psychic Phenomenon', she was one of my best students. Although I must admit, somewhat eccentric. When she discovered that I was experiencing a high rate of success, treating people with chronic disorders..."*** He pauses to clarify. ***"Substance abuse, smoking, you know. Well, she asked me if I'd be interested in using hypnosis to regress one of her clients."*** Doctor Shay pauses, and then continues. ***"So, I gave it a try and found the whole experience totally exhilarating! Voila', here I am. I suppose I've become kind of a prospector of the human mind. What I mean is, I've discovered a tool that can be used to dig out memories of past lives that people have lived. Or at least, believe, they've lived. Often the results are startling as well as beneficial."***

Paul asks, ***"Ever have any negative results?"***

Doctor Shay answers, ***"Not negative in a serious sense. Occasionally a patient suffers a degree of guilt or even disgust about how they acted in the past. It's not that they regret our sessions together, it's that they sometimes regret past actions. Actions that they are now unable to go back and change, do you understand?"*** Paul nods.

Doctor Shay continues, ***"It's important to me, that I evaluate each potential subject, before I begin. I need to be confident about that person's inner strength. Most of my best results are with people who understand the past for what it is... the past."***

The Doctor studies Paul for a moment, before continuing, ***"That's why I agreed to meet with you today. I first need to know that you have an open mind, and a willingness to accept information about your past, knowing full well that you cannot change things that've already happened."***

Doctor Shay stands and scans the room with his head and eyes as if he is forming his explanation. Paul is hanging on every word as the Doctor paces.

Then Doctor Shay continues, ***"This is not to imply that information we obtain through hypnosis will not better your current life, in fact, in all probability it will! But each case is***

different, some individuals appear to have lived wonderful lives, coming away from the experience with nothing but positive feelings." He pauses. ***"Others? Not so much."***

The Doctor returns to his seat. Then he adds, ***"I'm just concerned, that's all. The nightmares that you've had, that's a lot to go through for anyone."*** Paul nods in agreement. ***"I guess what I'm saying is, knowledge is power, good or bad, it's a powerful force to deal with."***

Paul asks, ***"So, what's your prognosis Dr. Shay? Do we proceed or not?"***

Doctor Shay answers, ***"Paul, it's not for me to decide. I know by talking to you that you have a strong desire to resolve all of this. And it certainly appears that your cosmic alarm clock is ringing, but even though I speculate that you can handle it, the final decision must remain yours. I want you to think about that."***

Paul is looking intently into the Doctor's eyes, hanging onto every word. He looks away for a moment and with a serious face, bringing his hand up to squeeze his forehead with two fingers, while concentrating on what the Doctor has told him. He smiles, drops his hand, and turns back towards the Doctor. He's made a decision. ***"I really want to know!"***

The Doctor smiles and nods.

The Regis' Kitchen

Karen is fixing dinner; she's still in her hospital work clothes when Paul enters through the front door. He calls out to her. ***"Karen?"***

Karen answers, ***"In here, Honey."***

Paul enters the house, setting his briefcase on a small counsel table on a chair and his suit coat on the chair next to it. He walks into the kitchen, and hugs Karen from behind who is busy at the stove.

She twists her head around; kissing the air as an affectionate gesture, while she continues to prepare dinner. She asks, ***"Are things getting back to normal at work?"***

Paul is a little bit distant as he makes his way over to the kitchen table and takes a seat. He doesn't address his wife's question right away, as if trying to come up with a plausible answer. He finally laughs and adds, ***"Yeah, yeah. Like I wasn't even gone."***

There is a brief lull in the conversation and then Paul says, ***"I, uh, went to see that Doctor this afternoon... The one that the fortune teller recommended. He does past life hypnosis."***

Karen asks, ***"How does that work?"***

Paul realizes how absurd 'what he is about to say' is going to sound, but he wants to be honest with

Karen. He explains, ***"Dr. Shay takes, or regresses, a patient back-in-time using hypnosis to a life that they may have lived in the past. A few decades or maybe even thousands of years ago."***

Karen continues to cook dinner but manages to engage Paul in the conversation at hand. ***"I thought you didn't believe it all that stuff. What was it you said?"*** She pauses and then blurts out, ***"Oh yeah, 'Mumbo Jumbo'."***

Paul becomes slightly embarrassed, ***"Well, I didn't say that I'd never check it out."*** He pauses. ***"Anyway, I met Doctor Shay this afternoon. Michael. Dr. Shay, thinks that some hypnosis sessions might help me cope better, with the hallucinations that I've been having."***

Karen is listening but appears slightly indifferent as she walks over and removes a half-dozen carrots from the refrigerator. She gathers up a chopping board, a peeler, and a chef's knife, and walks over to the kitchen table where Paul is sitting. She places everything in front of him while he's talking, ***"Here, make yourself useful."***

Paul starts by peeling the carrots, and then cutting them into little pieces. Karen reaches over and picks up one of the carrots to munch on, while she makes her way back to the stove. With her cheeks full of chewed up carrot and looking somewhat like a chipmunk she manages to ask, ***"So, tell me. Did he have anything constructive to say, or do you think he a quack?"***

Paul frowns asking, ***"Quack?"***

Karen stops chewing, aware that Paul is now taking all of this Hypnosis stuff a little more seriously than she had thought. She tries to recover, ***"Well, I don't know. Maybe 'quack' is a poor choice of words."***

Paul is thinking. Then Karen tries to change the mood of their conversation, ***"So, what's this Michael like?"***

Paul becomes his regular confident self before answering, ***"He seems nice. Of course, we talked about the visions... and uh, I gathered that he agrees with Clara Nelson's analysis."***

Karen pauses and looks up with what remains of a chewed up a carrot sticking out of her mouth. She asks, ***"Clara Nelson?"***

Paul explains, ***"She was the woman telling fortunes at the party last week."***

Karen tilts her head to one side, a little sarcastically as if to say, 'I'm supposed to remember Clara Nelson?'

Paul continues, ***"Anyway, no, he's not a quack. In fact, during the day, he's a regular Medical Doctor. He only does these regressions parttime. Apparently this is a very***

specialized kind of thing?" He pauses. ***"It was because of Clara that he became involved with Past Life Regressions. She was one of his former students."***

Karen is surprised, ***"Is she a Medical Doctor too?"***

Paul tries to clarify, ***"No, no, she was a student in a class he taught last summer, at Pepperdine. Something about medical issues and their relationships to the Paranormal, specifically Past Life Regressions."***

Karen inquires, ***"Past Life what?"***

Paul corrects her, ***"Past Life Regressions."*** He pauses.

Karen asks, ***"How does that work?"***

Paul tries to explain, ***"Basically he hypnotizes people and takes them back in time to lives they've potentially lived before. While they're under, they relive, and hopefully remember details, about things that happened in those past lives."*** He pauses. ***"It's a process of unlocking the subconscious mind."***

Karen stops what she's doing, she looks up at Paul concerned. ***"Is it dangerous?"***

Paul doesn't know for sure, but he tries to answer his wife in a positive manner, ***"Well, not really?"***

Karen isn't buying his explanation and asks, ***"What's that supposed to mean?"***

Paul tries to put the issue to bed, ***"No. It's not dangerous."***

Karen relaxes and resumes what she was doing. Paul feels a little bit guilty about his answer. He adds, ***"As long as the person under Hypnosis has a strong emotional will. Then there's no problem."***

She looks up at Paul concerned again. ***"So, if I understand you correctly, some people don't react well?"***

Paul tries to explain the best that he can, ***"Well. Some individuals don't handle information about their past very well. Dr Shay said that some people did things that they regret. But because they can't change things, remorse can take over."***

Karen asks, ***"What about you?"*** She pauses. It's obvious that she loves Paul and doesn't want anything to happen to him. Then she says, ***"You think all of this, is going to be beneficial in some way. Especially after all that's happened. I mean, the nightmares and the hallucinations?"***

Paul stands and walks over to the back door and lets the dog out. He closes the door slowly and turns to address her. ***"I need to know. I need to find out."***

Karen smiles as she begins to understand Paul's strong will, and determination. She crosses the room and hugs him.

Dr. Shay's office, later that week

Paul is reclining on a couch; Doctor Shay is speaking in a slow and soft tone of voice to Paul who lays still with his eyes closed.

Dr. Shay is putting Paul into a deep hypnotic state of mind. ***"Even further now Paul, go back even further, to another step, another time, further and further back***..." The Dr. pauses, ***"... Can you tell me what you see now?"***

Paul begins to smile, ***"My Mother. I see my Mother. She's playing with me. I made a pickle and mayonnaise sandwich for lunch and she's kidding me about it."***

Dr. Shay asks, ***"How old are you Paul?"***

Paul's voice changes slightly to that of a little boy. ***"I'm seven."***

Dr. Shay asks, ***"Paul? I want you to try to go even further back now. It's 1949, the year you were born. You're feeling very relaxed Paul, very calm and relaxed. Now Paul, listen very carefully, I want you to go back five years... now ten years... now it's 1934 a time before you were born, will you do that for me Paul?"*** Paul slowly nods yes. ***"Paul? Try to picture what you're seeing now; can you***

describe it to me? Describe what you see Paul."

Paul seems to become a bit distressed; he moves his head from side to side, but he answers the doctor***, "Blackness, I see nothing but blackness, blackness all around me."*** He begins to moan. Paul starts to exhibit a little panic and the Doctor quickly attempts to calm him.

Dr. Shay tries to reassure Paul***, "Everything is all right Paul. I'm right here by your side. Now I want you to try to relax."*** He pauses. ***"That's good Paul. Take a deep breath and relax. That's right, good, good. Now I want you to try and visualize exactly what is happening. Can you describe what you're seeing?"***

Paul is silent for a moment. Struggling at first with the vision, and then he begins to explain, ***"I'm walking down a road. It's a very long and narrow road. There's trees on each side."***

Dr. Shay asks***, "Where is this road located, Paul?"***

Paul stiffens up and answers, ***"Paul? My name's not Paul!"***

Doctor Shay is taken back for a moment, and then he formulates a new approach, to find out what's going on in Paul's mind***. "Oh, yes, please***

forgive me, I've forgotten your name. Can you please tell me again?"

Paul responds in English but with a slight German accent, and in a very assertive manner, highly unlike his normal persona. ***"Goltz! Herman Goltz! You may call me Herr Goltz."***

Dr. Shay asks, ***"Herr Goltz, can you tell me where you are?"***

Herr Goltz has seemed to take over Paul's mind. He answers, ***"In the Motherland. Germany! Where else?"***

Dr. Shay says, ***"And what are you doing as we speak?"***

Goltz answers, ***"I am walking down my road. The road to my house? I'm headed home."***

The Doctor is silent, waiting for Paul/Goltz to continue. Goltz is silent for a moment then he smiles as if he sees something off in the distance.

He explains, ***"There's a woman. She's smiling and running towards me. She's got her arms open wide. It's Gretchen, my wife."***

#6 - "The Ugliest Images"

We're thrust into another place, a place within Paul's subconscious mind. A woman (Gretchen) is running towards Herr Goltz, she's smiling, waving her arms, and running faster and faster. As she approaches she speaks. ***"Welcome home, husband."***

She begins to hug a large, lean, soldier in his early thirties. The man is dressed in a world war II German uniform. They kiss and she finally releases her grasp. As she does, she reaches down, and picks up the smaller of two bags that the man had dropped to hug her.

He picks up the larger bag and he loops her free arm into his, and the two of them continue walking down the road together, towards a small but beautiful farm house.

Gretchen says, ***"Your sister's here."*** She rolls her eyes telegraphing a thought, that Herr Goltz's sister can be a 'hand-full'.

Herr Goltz says, ***"I hope she doesn't want to argue politics, or anything else?"***

Gretchen raises her eyebrows and tilts her head. Gretchen says, ***"Try to have some patience with her. She's a new breed of German, young and idealistic."***

Herr Goltz seems a little bit exasperated, ***"That's what I'm most concerned about. It's those twisted humanitarian ideas she has about the Jews. Animals like that, cannot be treated with human dignity!"***

He pauses while he formulates what he's about to say, ***"She has to learn to keep her ideas to herself! I'm not beyond the grasp of the SS. Someday I may not be able to protect her, especially If she continues to be so***

outspoken. Someday she might say the 'wrong thing' to the 'wrong person'."

Gretchen smiles and squeezes his hand with her own in support, as the two of them continue walking down the road towards their little house.

Gretchen tries to be encouraging, ***"Try not to worry, husband. As long as she's here I'll. try to encourage her to keep her opinions to herself. She knows the penalties involved for supporting Jews."***

Herr Goltz rolls his eyes, shakes his head, and musters up a smile. He pauses and stops walking with Gretchen and he looks longingly into Gretchen's eyes before speaking, ***"You're a good wife, Gretchen. It'll be nice to have this time to ourselves... away from the war. To be around my own breed of people is a real joy."***

Herr Golts' Home

Gretchen and Herr Goltz enter the well-manicured and elaborately decorated cottage. It's obvious that Herr Goltz's position has allowed him to landscape and furnish his home with the finest things the Third Reich can provide.

He sets his bag down alongside the one Gretchen was carrying and takes off his military cap and his long overcoat draping both over the back of a chair next to a small table.

Gretchen is so, so, happy. She exclaims, ***"Look Ingrid, your father's home!"***

Sonya, Herman's sister, joins the family from a room in the rear of the home. Ingrid runs up to her father and he stoops to pick up the little ten year old girl.

He holds her tight, smiling as he swings her from side to side. The little girl is very excited to see her father again. Ingrid shouts out with glee, ***"Daddy, daddy!"***

Goltz says, ***"And how's my little princess? Have you been giving your Mother a bad time? Or have you been behaving?"***

Ingrid responds, ***"Behaving."***

Herr Goltz sets her down, pats her on the head and then stands erect. He looks his sisters way with a somewhat somber face. His sister, Sonya, breaks eye contact and takes another sip of her wine, lifting her glass high into the air as if to toast. She says, ***"Welcome home, Brother."***

Herr Goltz walks over to his sister. He musters up a half grin. Then he asks sarcastically, ***"And what about you, have you been a good girl?"***

Sonya's mood swings towards being happy to see her brother again, despite their political differences. She hugs him and Gretchen is pleased that she's at least trying to get along, for a change.

Gretchen interrupts, ***"Well, OK everyone. Let's move into the dining room."*** She glances at her husband. ***"I have a nice home cooked meal waiting since two o'clock my love."***

The Goltz Dining Room

Herr Goltz, Gretchen, Ingrid, and Sonya are just coming to the end of a lavish meal. We are immediately aware of the beautiful decor of this room, the eating utensils, plates, etc. There is no doubt that Herr Goltz is a high ranking officer in the German military.

Herr Goltz has since changed into civilian clothes. He leans back and pats his stomach. Before saying, ***"It's been some time since I had a meal like that."*** He looks at his wife, ***"Thank you my love."*** He reaches across the table where his wife is sitting and pats her hand in appreciation. She smiles and thanks him with a nice smile and a nod.

Sonya's face turns sour as she works hard to finish off her second glass of wine. Her outward appearance indicates that she's probably consumed too much. She speaks up brazenly, ***"So, tell me, brother."*** She pauses. ***"What do you think the Jews are eating for their Christmas dinner?"***

Gretchen is not pleased, ***"Sonya! Don't you think you've had enough wine?"***

Herr Goltz pats Gretchen's hand again, indicating that everything is under control. He smiles and looks at his daughter. ***"Ingrid, why don't you go up to your room and play?"***

Ingrid is disappointed and protests, ***"But Daddy, I want to have some dessert!"***

Herr Goltz smiles at his daughter, and being the tower of patience, he says, ***"Do as daddy says, and I'll bring you a big piece of apple strudel later, alright? And if you do as I say, I'll have a little surprise with me, OK?"***

Ingrid asks, ***"A present?"***

Herr Goltz smiles and nods, ***"Yes. Now do as I ask."***

His little girl smiles and leaves the table. Herr Goltz waits until he is sure that she is out of hearing range before he speaks.

#7 - "State of Hate"

He turns towards his half-drunk sister and frowns. ***"Why do you always defy me in front of my family?"***

She smiles, and looking away, reaches for more wine from the bottle. Gretchen stands up and begins to clear away the dishes. As she does, she intercepts the wine bottle and walks away with it and the other things, headed for the kitchen. Sonya is put off by Gretchen's action, but tries to laugh it off, as she tried to answer her brother's question. ***"Defy you, Brother? I don't defy***

you!" She glares at him. ***"I only defy what you stand for. The so-called 'Master Race,' that's the ideology that I reject. So don't take things so seriously."***

She chuckles and adding insult to injury she adds, ***"Why you're just a puppet, I understand this. You're just a pawn in Hitler's insane plan."***

As a loyalist, Herr Goltz is obviously maddened by her abusive comments. He struggles to remain in control of his emotions as he responds to her ridicule. ***"If you were anyone else but my sister, I'd... "***

#08 - "Sister's Shame"

Sonya interrupts, ***"You'd what? Have me put to death?"***

Herr Goltz is speechless. Just then Gretchen comes back in the room to witness the last of the fireworks between the two siblings. She has not heard everything, but she can imagine what has happened, so she speaks out to Sonya. ***"Why do you spoil the moment by insulting your brother?"***

Sonya rejects Gretchen's interpretation of what just happened. She speaks out in an attempt to defend herself. ***"Is that true? Do I insult you Brother?"***

She stands up with her now half empty wine glass, and strolls around the room, touching all the valuable furnishings with her free hand as she continues. ***"Does the truth, 'insult' you brother?"*** Then Sonya directs a question to Gretchen. ***"How about you, Sister-in-law? Are you 'insulted' when you hear the truth?"***

Gretchen stops cold and looks at Sonya, using her hands to plead silently for Sonya to stop this foolishness. Sonya addresses Gretchen again. Almost demanding an answer. ***"Ask him what he does for Hitler!"***

#09 - "His Job"

Sonya walks over to where Herr Goltz is sitting, she leans down on the table on one hand, placing her face about two inches from his and staring into his eyes, she asks rhetorically. ***"Why don't you tell your wife the reason that you're known as the "MASTER OF MISERY?"***

Gretchen cannot cope, she shakes her head at this all too common situation and leaves the room frustrated.

Herr Goltz responds to his sister's badgering. ***"I have a sworn allegiance to der Fuhrer, a duty to rid the pestilence from the Motherland."***

Sonya sets her glass down, stands erect and applauds him as if he's just given a significant speech. ***"Bravo Herr Goltz, bravo!"***

Herr Goltz points at her, shaking his index finger. ***"The animals I deal with are being eradicated removed from German society, because they are an inferior race that hinders the future of***

our people. The Jews will no longer suppress the German people in any way, and when Germany wins this war they will all be eliminated from the face of the Earth!"

#08 - "Sister's Shame"

Sonya in blatant defiance, strolls the room again, keeping her eyes locked on her brother's. She says sarcastically, ***"Look at all the beautiful things in this room. Ten years ago, you had nothing! Suddenly now..."*** She pauses and smiles waving her hand. ***"... Well? Look! See for yourself."***

Herr Goltz is so angry he can hardly contain himself as he listens to his sister's accusations. As she abuses him verbally.

Finally, he tries to defend himself, ***"Everything in this house was given to me, gifts from der Fuhrer for outstanding service to the Third Reich!"***

Sonya immediately jumps in, ***"And just where do you think these things came from? Did your Fuhrer buy them? Maybe he made them? Maybe he traded something of value for them?"*** She laughs at her little joke, and pauses.

#09 - "His Job"

She moves closer to her brother taking a seat next to him at the table. She moves in so close that he can smell her hot, wine tainted breath, on his face.

She asks, ***"Well? Tell me how the Nazis came by all these riches? How, brother? Explain that!"***

Herr Goltz has heard enough. ***"You're drunk!"***

Sonya ties to defend her point of view, ***"Sure, I'm drunk all right! Drunk with disgust! I'm disgusted with the way my own flesh and blood can abuse another human being, and still sleep at night!"***

#10 - "Inhuman"

She walks back to her side of the table and sits down. She seems to be feeling a little bit defeated. ***"I'm ashamed of myself, I'm ashamed to be known as a Goltz, but most of all, I'm ashamed of my country."***

Herr Goltz has finally heard enough out of his anti-Nazi sister. He says, ***"Look, I'm not interested in your drunken opinions of our great country's political struggle. Furthermore, I am not interested in your opinions of my work! It's none of your business what I do... politically or otherwise! I have a job to do, and I answer to no one, but der Fuhrer."*** Herr Goltz is obviously letting off steam at this point. He is pissed off that his sister is insulting him in his own home. He adds, ***"And another thing. This is my home. You're a guest here. While you're here, I want you to show a little respect."***

Sonya is only half listening; this irritates him even more. And he raises his voice, ***"DO YOU UNDERSTAND ME?"***

Sonya looks at him, with a cynical stare. She answers him, ***"YES! YES! YES! Of course, I understand! I'm to keep silent. I'm to stand by and say nothing! Don't worry Brother; you have nothing to worry about from me. I won't spread your dirty little secrets."***

Sonya has earned the dominant position in the discussion. Realizing this, Goltz slams his fist down on the table and stands. Getting his sister's attention, he adds, ***"My job is to effectively dispose of the opposition"*** Then he almost becomes hysterical… ***"THIS IS WAR AND THAT'S THE WAY IT IS! DO YOU HEAR ME, DO YOU?"***

#11 - "The Doctor's Concern"

Dr. Shay's Office

Paul is still lying on the couch; Doctor Shay begins to wake him from the hypnotic trance.

Dr. Shay instructs Paul, ***"Paul I want you to go forward in time now, I want you to pass into your current life, the life where you're known as Paul Regis. On my count of three you will awake. One, you're starting to wake up. Two, you're feeling wonderful and***

rejuvenated. And three your back to the present time."

As the Doctor pauses on that thought for a moment, Paul opens his eyes and responds with a big smile. The doctor asks, ***"How 'ya feeling?"***

It's the first time Doctor Shay has attempted to speak to Paul Regis in over an hour, he wonders for a moment, who, will respond. He asks again, ***"Paul?"***

Paul answers right away, ***"Yes?"***

Paul stretches, and looks at Dr. Shay who's smiling at him. ***"How do you feel?"***

Paul answers, ***"A little sleepy, but otherwise good!"***

Dr. Shay says, ***"Look. Why don't you just lie here awhile and rest for a few minutes OK? When you're feeling a little more energetic we'll talk."***

The Doctor gets up and leaves the room. ***"I'll be right next door, when you're feeling wide awake again, please join me."***

Paul smiles and nods. The Doctor shuts a small tape recorder off, then leaves the room. He is careful to close the door quietly. All we hear is a faint click.

Dr. Shay's private office

We're looking over the shoulder of Doctor Shay, who is standing at his office window looking outside. Paul Regis enters the room and takes a seat. Doctor Shay turns and smiles at Paul and then takes a seat behind his desk.

Dr. Shay says, ***"Paul. I'm simply fascinated, what else can I say? I am truly at a loss for words."***

Paul smiles. ***"So, things turned out well?"***

Dr. Shay says, ***"Well? I should say so. My God man! You were there; I think once you hear the tape, you'd have to agree with me when I describe this session as over-the-top! Even that would be under estimating the circumstances a little!"*** The doctor pauses. ***"Paul, I've never had a subject recall with such clarity and detail. Are you aware that for a while, you actually adopted another complete personality?"***

Doctor Shay stands and begins to pace his office. Then he adds, ***"Communicating with Paul Regis became impossible! Frankly, you had me a little worried for a while."***

Paul inquires, ***"Worried?"***

Dr. Shay explains, ***"Yes, I was beginning to wonder how I was going to bring you back to the present. Your other personality was very strong. You became a Nazi commander by***

the name of Herman Goltz; and I would speculate that this "Goltz" wants to "clear the slate", so to speak. There wasn't a whole lot of room in there for Paul Regis."

He pauses. ***"Your present life has opened the door for your past to come through. Each life spent here on Earth is an opportunity to correct past mistakes. This other you... Herman Goltz... wants to clear his consciousness through you, through Paul Regis. Kind of an elaborate confession if you will."***

Paul is very curious. He asks, ***"So, what about the nightmares and hallucinations, do they come from this Goltz person?"***

Dr. Shay explains, ***"Well it's still kind of early to be establishing any facts, but if I had to make an educated guess. I think I'd have to say... yes! I'm not exactly sure how I know this, but I'd bet that most of your nightmares and visions might disappear after this session."***

Paul is apprehensive, and asks, ***"But no guarantees?"***

Dr. Shay says, "I wish I had all the answers, but I can't promise anything. I've never had a patient react like you. And I'd like to continue. Now I don't expect an answer right away, I want you to think about it, but even if it's a 'no', I'd still appreciate at least one more session with you."

Paul is game, but also slightly apprehensive, ***"Just as long as I don't end up as this other character. That would really piss my wife off."***

Dr. Shay laughs. Then he explains, ***"I understand your concern, but in my professional opinion, I don't think there's any real chance of that happening. However, there might be a danger I'm not aware of. That's why the final decision must be left up to you. You need to think about this. Maybe talk it over with your wife too?"***

Paul explains, ***"I think Karen would want me to continue. I can't live with this, and I... We... Need some answers."***

Dr. Shay responds, ***"All right, Paul. I just want to say, that I'm more concerned about your availability, over and above any payment. I consider this case a hallmark, and I'm privileged, to be a part of it!"***

Paul tries to be accommodating, ***"As long as I have some advanced notice, I'm pretty much available."***

Dr. Shay smiles, ***"Wonderful!"***

#12 – "Lunch with Jerry"

Outside Patio at a Restaurant

Paul is being served a drink, he thanks the waiter, takes a sip, and then spots Jerry Spaulding who he has been expecting. He flags Jerry over to his table with an outstretched arm. Paul smiles and stands up holding out his hand to shake. ***"Hi Jerry. Glad you could make it."***

As Jerry takes his seat, he asks, ***"How's Karen?"***

Paul answers, ***"She's doing quite well Jerry! How about Michelle?"***

Jerry answers, ***"She's fine. But, always talking about weddings, what else? You know women."***

The waiter appears. ***"Will the gentleman be having lunch with us today?"***

Jerry answers, ***"Yes, thank you."***

With that, the waiter unfolds a menu and hands it to Jerry. Then he asks, ***"Can I get you something to drink in the meantime?"***

Jerry answers, ***"Yeah, uh, I'll have a shot of Peppermint Schnapps over ice."*** The Waiter nods and then he asks. ***"Would you like to order now, or shall I come back?"***

Paul speaks up, ***"The Scampi here is great!"***

Jerry makes his decision, ***"Fine, I'll try that."***

The waiter says, ***"Wonderful, Scampi all around then. I'll be right back with your drink sir, and your salads."*** The waiter leaves.

Jerry asks, ***"So, I have it on good authority that you're seeing that old witch."***

Paul laughs, ***"You must mean, Clara?"***

Jerry seems surprised and trying to be funny he says, **"I didn't realize that you two were on a first name basis. Don't tell me... She found out that you've got crystal balls?"**

Paul laughs at Jerry's humor. ***"Actually, I haven't seen her since the party."*** The waiter brings the drinks and two salads. Then Paul continues, ***"Although, I am seeing a doctor friend of her's. Someone she recommended at the party."***

Jerry asks, ***"A shrink?"***

Paul grins and adds, ***"Very funny Jerry, but No. He's a regular MD. We just started working together."***

Jerry seems shocked and says, ***"You serious?"***

Paul smiles, ***"Like a heart attack."***

Jerry's curious and asks, ***"I don't get it. At the party I had to drag you in the kitchen to catch that old bag's act. Now you're telling me that you're a regular customer."*** While Jerry pauses.

Paul sips his drink, then he corrects Jerry, "***Well, I'm not exactly her customer. I'm just seeing a doctor friend of hers."***

Then Jerry asks, ***"Why the sudden change of heart?"***

Paul clarifies, ***"Remember those dreams I told you about?"*** Jerry nods. ***"Well, Clara speculated that one of my past lives was attempting to reach out to me, through my subconscious. That's when she recommended this doctor friend of hers that does regression hypnosis."*** Jerry's listening but can hardly believe what he's hearing. Paul continues, ***"Doctor Michael Shay. He's actually quite an interesting fellow."***

Jerry seems concerned and asks, ***"Is this guy a real doctor?"***

Paul answers excitedly, ***"Yes! He's a Physician at West Side Hospital. This hypnosis thing is only a sideline."***

Jerry asks sarcastically, ***"You sure you don't mean sideshow?"***

Paul frowns, ***"I'm serious Jerry!"***

Jerry adds, ***"Well, you have to admit; it's a little "much," coming from you Paul. Mr. upper-middle class guy who was a staunch skeptic a few weeks ago."***

Paul looks a little bit guilty before answering, ***"I know. I know. Look; I'm not about to join a***

religious cult and move to the hills to drink the Kool-Aid, I can assure you."

Jerry says a bit sarcastically, ***"Well that's encouraging buddy! And Karen? How's she taking all of this?"***

Just then the waiter brings the entrees'. There's a brief pause in the conversation while the two men get ready to eat. Then Paul tries to answer Jerry's question, ***"Like you at first. But, uh, now I think she understands my motivation."***

Jerry asks, ***"How much is all of this gonna cost you?"***

Paul answers positively, ***"Dr. Shay's providing his services for free. Look, I realize all of this sounds a little weird. It's still weird to me!"***

Jerry smiles as he tries to respond, ***"I'm just concerned, that's all. I mean, one minute you're a pillar of stone and the next, you're packing for a trip to the Twilight Zone."***

Paul looks at Jerry and realizes he's only trying to be funny. He begins to laugh at his joke. But he realizes that Jerry does have a point.

Paul still laughing, ***"That's good Jerry, you know you can be very funny!"*** Paul continues to laugh.

Jerry says, ***"Are you laughing or crying?"*** The two men are laughing together as they both begin to eat their lunch.

#13 – "Have Mercy"

Regis Master Bedroom

Paul and Karen are sound asleep. Paul begins to show signs that he's dreaming. His lips start moving as if he's speaking to someone.

We're slowly drawn into Paul's dream, suddenly we're in a train yard, it's misty and damp. In the background we see several boxcars.

In the foreground we see a large group of people standing around just waiting... men, women, and small children. Mingling within this group are several Nazi soldiers with weapons.

Herr Goltz enters from the right with two other soldiers at his side. He scans the crowd and seems to be singling out certain individuals, and couples.

He walks carefully by as he studies the prisoners', he pauses, and points to a couple in their sixties indicating that they should move to the left.

A much younger man, their grandson, attempts to stay with them. Herr Goltz motions to a soldier standing close by that he doesn't want the young man joining them, and the soldier steps between the boy and his grandparents.

The boy resists and attempts to stick with what appears to be his grandparents. The Grandmother at this point is attempting to hold onto his shoulder grasping the young man's coat.

Herr Goltz is amused at this act of desperation and steps through the crowd, over to where the trio is standing. All activity stops as he stands in front of this ongoing scenario, he looks at the young man.

Herr Goltz addresses the young man, ***"Do you wish to be with your people?"***

The young man, thinking that he has struck a note of compassion within his captor, smiles and nods yes. Slowly and methodically Herr Goltz draws his sidearm from his holster, the boy begins to struggle and is quickly subdued by two soldiers.

Herr Goltz smiles, turns suddenly, and without warning, kills the boys grandparents on the spot. The young man is shocked at his brutality, and lunges towards his grandmother's body trying to hold it up off the ground. He begins to wail with grief. Herr Goltz smiles. With the pistol still smoking he holsters the weapon. He looks at the young man and asks, ***"Do you still wish to be with your people?"***

The young man fighting back tears screams something in Yiddish at Herr Goltz. Goltz does not understand and leans to one of his soldiers. ***"What did he say?"*** The soldier is reluctant to speak. He waits for an answer. then asks him again, ***"Well?"***

The soldier seems reluctant to answer, but finally does, ***"He said, someday, somehow... I will hunt you down and kill you, you Nazi scum!"***

Herr Goltz is infuriated by this young Jew's threat and snaps his head back pointing his pistol at the boy's temple. He pauses, regains his composure, knowing full well that the boy probably will not live long enough to carry out his threat.

He laughs out loud, re-holsters his weapon and turns away. The young man attempts to jump him but is beaten back by the soldiers. Herr Goltz's begins to laugh hysterically, his face seems to distort, his laughter begins to echo. It stops suddenly and Herr Goltz's face becomes filled with terror, as he suddenly finds himself standing alone on a dark, wet, empty cobblestone street.

He suddenly begins to sweat and turns looking at every shadow. From behind a post the young man steps out. He raises a pistol and Herr Goltz starts to walk backwards pleading with his hands silently, then he turns and runs... shots ring out and ricochet' off the walls of the buildings he passes. It's the young man that is laughing now, chasing Herr Goltz.

As the young man steps from behind each corner we see him age progressively. First a little older then middle aged; then in his early sixties, at this point he has a beard, glasses, and he's much heavier.

He stops laughing, raises his pistol and shoots... again... and again... then he laughs hysterically, it echoes, his face distorts as the nightmare progresses, louder and louder!

Suddenly Paul wakes up. He's in a cold sweat but tries not to wake Karen; he gets up slowly making his way to the bathroom. He carefully closes the door, putting on the light, and he bends over the sink, splashing cold water in his face trying to shake the dream.

#14 – "The Chamber"

With wet eyes he gropes with his right hand for a towel. Suddenly in the reflection of the mirror we see the fat bearded man, smiling, and holding a pistol that is pointed directly at Paul.

Paul is terrified; he spins around only to find nothing. He gasps!

Dr. Shay's office the next week

Paul is laying on the Doctor's couch. He been describing the recent nightmare. He finishes up his story, ***"I spun around, and he was gone."***

Doctor Shay ponders Paul's story. Then he asks, ***"Tell me, Paul; were the images crystal clear, like previous visions?"***

Paul is thinking, then he answers, ***"Uh, no. The previous images were lifelike, I mean they were as if I was really there. The other night was more like a regular dream."*** He interrupts himself to clarify. ***"Except that image in the mirror, that was as real as it gets."***

Doctor Shay asks, ***"This boy, the one that aged as you went along, does he have a name?"***

Paul struggles to remember, ***"I don't recall hearing any name, or at least I don't remember any name in particular."***

The Doctor begins to pace. Then he asks, ***"I don't understand why this young man hasn't materialized in any of our sessions before? At least you've never mentioned him before."*** He pauses. ***"Any speculation?"*** Paul shakes his head. The doctor continues, ***"Could be, were dealing with some kind of Cross-Imaging."***

Paul asks, ***"What's that?"***

Doctor Shay tries tom explain, ***"It's rare, but it surfaces in certain cases from time to time. It's when two, usually unrelated images, connect themselves through the subconscious mind."*** He pauses. ***"Possibly this bearded man is an old client of yours?"*** Paul shakes his head no. Then the doctor continues, ***"Well, I'll add it to my notes, who knows? Maybe it'll become more clear later? Look, I have an opening on Thursday. Can you drop by?"*** He moves to his desk, opens an appointment book, and asks, ***"Would, 5:45 in the afternoon be ok with you?"***

Paul smiles, **"Unless my receptionist has already set something up, I think that'll be fine. I'll ask her to confirm things."**

The Doctor seems to be off in deep thought. Paul gets up to leave, and then he asks, "Guess I wasn't much help today, huh?"

Doctor Shay's day dream is interrupted by Paul's question, he answers, ***"On the contrary, any new developments only serve to enhance the project, besides... "*** The Doctor pauses and then smiles confidently. ***"... I received some very interesting news today."*** Paul's interest is peaked, and he leans in to listen. The doctor continues, ***"I enlisted the services of an old friend of mine, who works at the library. She did a little background research on our friend, Herr Goltz!"***

Paul perks right up.

The doctor raises his two hands in a gesture of slowing down Paul's possible excitement, ***"Now don't get too excited, OK? I really didn't want to mention this until I had more time to review the information thoroughly. Anyway, it seems that not only did Herr Goltz actually live, but he had one hell of a nasty reputation to boot! According to my contact, Goltz died at the wheel of his sports car. The accident happened in Switzerland, long after the war ended."*** He pauses. ***"Almost six years before you were born. I suppose that rules out any connection between the bearded man and the accident that killed Goltz?"***

Paul is astonished at this new development. The Doctor is astonished at the events that have unfolded over the past few weeks. He looks at Paul as a wonderment. ***"Well... I'm sure it'll all***

come together as we continue. I'll see you Thursday, right?"

Paul puts on a happy face, as he says, ***"Wouldn't miss it for the world!"***

Westside Hospital's Cafeteria

Doctor Shay is eating lunch with two other physicians from the Hospital. It's apparent that the Doctor to his left is Female and the Doctor to his right is Male. The conversation is already in progress.

The Female Doctor asks, ***"That's very interesting Michael. And you say there's facts?"***

Dr. Michael Shay answers, "***Yes. There's no question that these events occurred, historically speaking. Herr Goltz actually lived. In fact, he was a major element in creating the holocaust***." He pauses. ***"Goltz was some sort of protégé to Mengele."***

The male doctor asks, "And you're absolutely sure, beyond a shadow of a doubt?"

Doctor Shay is a little frustrated by this question, and he answers to substantiat4 his claim, ***"Yes. I have copies of documents dating back to the organization of the concentration camps."*** Doctor Shay leans forward looking back and forth between the two other physicians for some sort of validation. Then he adds, ***"I cannot***

prove that Paul wasn't deliberately or unintentionally exposed to this historical information beforehand. I guess it's possible that he did, although I think Paul would have told me."

The male doctor asks, ***"Paul?"***

Doctor Shay is deep in thought as he hastily answers. ***"Yes. Paul Regis, my patient."***

The female doctor interrupts, ***"Oh, Oh."***

Doctor Shay is deep in thought when he notices the comment from the female doctor. He asks, ***"Huh?"***

The female doctor adds, ***"Careful Michael. You don't want to violate patient confidentiality."***

Michael realizes that exposing a patient's name is not Kosher, but he quickly realizes that she is not trying to be serious, and is only ribbing him, he smiles.

Paul's Office – Thursday AM

Paul is seated at his desk. His intercom buzzes. He answers. ***"Yes?"***

BARBARA (the receptionist) ***"I have Doctor Shay on line four. Are you available, or should I take a message?"***

Paul anxiously says, ***"No, no... I'll take it. Thanks Barbara."***

He punches in the appropriate phone line and answers the call. ***"Michael, how are you?"***

We see Doctor Shay standing alongside his desk. In the background several police are walking around, taking photos, and logging evidence from his office. The office has obviously being ransacked and it's in shambles.

Michael is not happy, as he tries to explain, ***"Look, Paul, I'm afraid we've had a bit of a problem over here, I'm going to have to take a rain check on today's appointment."*** He looks around the wrecked office and reveals, ***"I was vandalized last night, and they really made a mess of things."***

Paul says, ***"I'm sorry to hear that. Are you alright?"***

Michael answers, ***"Yeah, I'm fine. "I haven't had a chance to look things over but at this point who knows what they wanted, drugs I guess? Anyway, give me a day or two and I'll call you, OK?"***

Paul responds, ***"Sure, that'll be fine, Michael, take care."***

Paul hangs up the receiver. He's bewildered at this turn of events.

Upper-class Residential Neighborhood

Looking down a tree lined street, headlights approach and turn into the driveway to our right, as we move in closer we can see the name on the mailbox - Mr. & Mrs. Josef Hausmann.

#15 – "Russell's Home"

Inside the Hausmann Home

A young college-aged man enters and walks to the rear of the home, entering the kitchen. It's Russell Hausmann the Hausmann's son. When he reaches the kitchen, he runs into his mother.

He greets his mother, ***"Hi Mom."***

Mrs. Hausmann is preparing dinner and when she spots her son, she asks, ***"Have you eaten?"***

Russel answers, ***"Yeah, I had a late lunch at school."*** He sets his books down, get a glass from the cupboard, milk from the refrigerator and pours himself a glass which he promptly drinks halfway, before pulling out a chair so he can sit at the kitchen table. Then he takes a big breath, smiles, and adds, ***"Finley gave me an A on my final."***

He lets the news slip, to catch his Mother's reaction, then sits back smiling. His mother stops stops what she's doing and smiles back. She's obviously very proud of her son. She says, ***"Russell, that's wonderful. Have you told your father?"***

Russell gets up and walks over to a cookie jar and removes a couple of cookies. Then he returns to his seat at the table. He responds, ***"No. Not yet. Is he upstairs?"***

Mrs. Hausmann is already back at work but casually answers, ***"Uh, huh. He's in the study."***

Russell gulps the last of his milk down and walks towards the stairway with his mouth filled with cookie.

The Study

Russell knocks and slowly opens the study door. Across the room we see a large man seated at a desk, he looks up. It's Josef Hausmann, the same man that Paul Regis saw in the reflection of his bathroom mirror. The same man trying to kill Herr Goltz in the dream.

Josef hastily closes a book that he was looking at. He acts a little bit like he has been caught doing something wrong.

Russell speaks up, ***"Oh hi dad, am I interrupting anything important?"***

The elder Hausmann answers a little nervously. ***"No Russell, come in, I, uh, I was just going over some of my paperwork, come in, please. What's up?"*** With one hand on the closed book, the elder Hausmann flags his son over to a chair with his free hand. ***"Sit down, please."*** Russell is full of energy as he takes a seat in front of his Father's desk. He smiles with excitement before revealing the facts, ***"Professor Finley's final? I***

passed!" He pauses for emphasis. ***"With an A no less!"***

The elder Hausmann smiles proudly, he stands up, and walks to Russell's side of the desk. Russell stands up to meet him, and the Elder Hausmann hugs his son.

Josef says, ***"I'm very proud of you son."*** He holds his son's shoulders and squeezes them with his two hands. He's very pleased. ***"So, may I assume that this means a scholarship?"***

Russell acts confident 'polishing his knuckles on his chest', in a playful manner. ***"Yes. I'm fairly certain of that now."***

The elder Hausmann, still smiling, takes a seat in the chair next to Russell's. ***"Then you'll have to start making some decisions about which college you'll be attending?"***

Russell stands up. He's thinking as he walks over to the window behind his father's desk, he looks out before answering. ***"Well. I may take a little time off before I decide that."***

The elder Hausmann is a little concerned. ***"Do you think that's wise Russell? I mean, you might lose the momentum. You run the risk of losing interest in college altogether. It's fairly common for that to happen when students take too much time off to 'find themselves', you know?"***

Russell moves to his Father's desk and sits down in his father's chair, placing his hand on top of the book his father was just looking at minutes before he arrived in his father's study. Josef becomes nervous and tries to stay on the subject of Russell's schooling. ***"What I mean is, it's easy to lose interest once you're away from the whole educational mechanism for too long."***

Russell answers, ***"Yeah, I suppose you're right, but I'm just talking about the summer months. I was thinking about going to Europe until school starts again in the fall."***

Russell pats the top of the book with his hand, almost inconspicuously. The elder Hausmann is uncomfortable with this. He steps back around to the business side of his desk and reaches over, sliding the book out from under Russell's hand. The sweat beads up on his forehead. He tries to smile. ***"Well... you're a bright boy, I'm sure you'll do the right thing when the time comes."***

Russell now senses that something is bothering his dad, as he watches his dad draw the book in closer to him. Almost as if he is trying to hide or protect it.

Russell stands up, turns, and takes a seat on the corner of his father's desk. His father immediately returns to his desk chair clutching the book. Russell can sense that something is amiss, and he reaches over and takes the book from his dad.

The elder Hausmann reluctantly lets go, leaning back in his chair, looking quite defeated. He rubs his face with his hands, sighing. Russell sets the book down on the desk and opens it.

#16 – "Ashamed"

He begins to scan the horrible photographs in what is obviously a book about Nazi Germany and the concentration camps. Russell is horrified at the photos.

Russell is shocked at what he sees. He says, ***"Jesus Christ! Where the hell did this come from?"***

The elder Hausmann is starting to calm down now that 'the cat is out of the bag'. He tries to explain, ***"It's where my parents... Your grandparents, were murdered."***

Russell looks at his Father bewildered. He wants to know more. ***"I thought you told me Grandpa and Grandma died in a fire? I don't understand."***

The elder Hausmann gets up and begin pacing the floor while his son turns the pages of the photo album. Finally, he tries to give a reasonable answer to Russell, ***"Yes... I did. I guess I didn't want you to know the details, especially when you were younger. That's why I tried to cover up everything."*** The elder Hausmann is frustrated at himself, unable to provide Russell with an adequate answer to his valid question. So, he says, "I don't know, Russell. It was just too horrible to share with you.

Russell reacts, ***"Goddamn Dad. I'm shocked that you actually kept those photos all these years. Who the fuck took those pictures anyway?"***

Josef answers right away, ***"The Germans documented all of their atrocities. I can only imagine that they wanted a record of what they did to eradicate us Jews."***

Russell asks, ***"How did you get them?"***

Josef explains, ***"Look son; I've been tracking the Nazis that were responsible for those crimes, most of my life. There's a group of us survivors back in Israel, and with the proper evidence, they've been able to bring many of those responsible to trial."***

Russell asks, ***"Is that why you keep them?"*** He pauses. ***"Because they're fucking horrible."***

Josef answers timidly, ***"I keep them because I never want to forget what happened."***

Russell is silent as he continues to turn the pages of the book. Each photo is another example of death and misery. Josef stands and paces the room. Russell turns a page; and we see a photograph of three people next to a box car. The elder Hausmann points at the picture and begins to tell Russell the whole story. ***"This photograph***

is your grandparents and me together. It's the last photograph taken of them."

Russell rubs the side of his face as he ponders this turn of events. He can sense the high level of emotions that are running through his father's mind. He asks, ***"Tell me what happened?"***

The elder Hausmann walks to the window and looks out, before he begins to relate the story. ***"When we arrived at the camp we were surrounded by soldiers and held in a group until the Commanding Officer arrived, Herman Goltz. He walked through the crowd and picked out the strongest men for work details. Your Grandfather was not in the best of health and was ordered to stand to one side with the women, Grandmother was at his side. I, uh, I tried to stay with them and uh, because of my efforts they were shot."***

Russell asks, ***"By the guards?"***

The elder Hausmann turns and walks back over to the open book on his desk. He flips through the pages until he comes to a newspaper article, which shows a large military photo of Herr Goltz. He points at it as he tries to answer, ***"No. By this man, Herr Goltz! Many died that afternoon. The next day the Nazis started burning bodies. It was late October. The fires burned for weeks; well into November, later they would call them "The Fires of Fall."***

The photograph of Herr Goltz lays open in the book. The Herr Goltz photo slowly transforms into the face of Paul Regis, and then back to Herr Goltz.

The Regis Home

We're at the front door of the Regis home, Doctor Michael Shay and another man are knocking on the front door.

Paul answers and greets Doctor Shay, and the another man, ***"Hello Michael, please come in?"***

Doctor Shay says, ***"I'm sorry to have to bother you at home, Paul."***

Once inside Paul closes the front door. He motions with his open hand that they should come into the living room. As the three men take seats, Karen enters the room. Paul says, ***"No problem Michael. By the way, this is my wife Karen. Karen this is Doctor Michael Shay."***

Michael smiles and nods, ***"So nice to meet you. Ah, this is Sergeant William Olsen."*** The sergeant nods to both Paul and Karen.

Michael adds, ***"I uh, I wanted to come along because I didn't want you to think that you were in any kind of trouble."***

Sergeant Olsen chimes in, ***"No, I can vouch for the Doc, this is strictly routine. I'd just like to ask you a few questions if that's all right?"***

Karen smiles and interrupts, ***"Would everyone like some coffee?"***

Sergeant Olsen smiles and confirms, ***"That would be Wonderful!"*** The Sergeant takes off his coat, and Karen is quick to take it from him. She hangs it up in the hall closet on her way into the kitchen.

Sergeant Olsen says, ***"Nice place you have here, Mr. Regis."***

Doctor Shay interrupts the pregnant pause following the Sergeant's compliment. Then he says, ***"Look, uh, Paul, I'm here because I feel that something bad is going to happen."*** Paul has a confused and worried look on his face. The Sergeant notices and he adds, ***"It's fairly obvious to me that you don't have a clue to why we're here, do you Mr. Regis?"***

Paul responds, ***"I can only speculate that it has something to do with the break-in at Michael's office?"***

The Sergeant smiles. Then he blurts out, ***"Bingo! Doctor Shay told me you were sharp. Look, uh, Mr. Regis I have to ask you this one question first, OK?"***

Paul nods. Michael leans back in his seat looking somewhat embarrassed at what Sergeant Olsen is about to ask Paul.

"Did you break into Doctor Shay's office and steal your file?"

Michael is shocked at the sergeant's brazen approach. He protests, ***"Jesus Christ, Sergeant!"***

Paul can't believe that he's a possible suspect and he is shocked. ***"What the fuck, Michael?"***

The sergeant repeats the question, ***"Did you break into Doctor Shay's office and yank your file?"***

Karen returns with a tray full of coffee cups, cream, sugar, and some spoons. She's heard the sergeant's question. She is amazed at all of this, and takes a seat, silently watching the scenario unfold. Paul is a little put out and answers. ***"That's absurd! What motivation would I have to do a stupid thing like that? If I wanted my file that bad I'm sure Michael would have happily given it to me willingly."***

Michael interrupts, ***"That's right! I would have."***

Sergeant Olsen concedes, ***"Yeah, well, I didn't think you took it, but I had to ask."***

Michael is upset that the sergeant asked, as a matter of principal. Karen also has a look on her face that telegraphs that she isn't too happy about the sergeant's line of questioning. Karen is a bit perturbed and asks, ***"Then why did you ask?"***

Sergeant Olsen answers, ***"It's my job, no offense intended Mame, I just have to ask, that's all."***

Karen not knowing either of these men and being slightly bent out of shape about the question, gets up and leaves the room.

The Sergeant addresses Paul, ***"I hope you'll express my apologies to your wife, but you folks have to understand that because the only thing missing from the Doc's office was your file, everything points to you."***

This is obviously the first Paul's heard about this. He snaps his head towards Michael and asks, ***"Do you think I stole my own file?"***

Michael answers, ***"No. Of course, not Paul. But, after a couple of days we discovered that the only thing missing was your file. We wouldn't have even discovered that it was missing, if it hadn't been for the fact that I was going to set up a new appointment for you, and your file was missing."***

Paul is little bit offended, ***"Well, I hope to God that you don't think I had anything to do with that Michael."***

Doctor Shay opens his hands (palms up) as he shakes his head no. Then he says, ***"No, of course not Paul! But the Sergeant insisted that we ask you about it. If I had my druthers I wouldn't have bothered you about this at all."***

Karen reenters the living room and takes a seat.

Sergeant Olsen obviously expects her to serve him his coffee. He brazenly asks Karen, ***"I'll take mine, Blond and Sweet!"***

He chuckles at his own somewhat crude humor; and continues talking with Paul. Karen doesn't like Olsen's tone, but pours him a cup anyway. Then, as long as she's doing it, she serves doctor Shay and Paul.

Then the sergeant says, ***"I'm curious Mr. Regis."*** Paul looks at him. He adds, ***"Why would anyone go to all that trouble, just to steal your file?"***

Paul is as stumped as Sergeant Olson, ***"I really don't know?"***

Sergeant Olsen says, ***"Well, one thing's for sure. It was an amateur!"***

Karen asks in a somewhat sarcastic tone, ***"How do you know that?"***

Sergeant Olsen says, ***"Because a professional would have stolen several files, maybe a handful from several drawers. You see, the thief, messed up the office to throw us off."*** He sips his cup of coffee before continuing, ***"That way we'd think it was vandalism, or we'd be looking for something else, not one little file. See, amateurs are nervous. They make stupid mistakes. For example, in an armed robbery? It's rare to even find bullets in a***

professional's gun. Amateurs start shooting if the temperature goes up."

Karen is smart and she concludes, "Somehow I get the feeling that there's more to this than a lost file?"

Sergeant Olsen smiles at Karen's powers of observation. ***"That's good, Ma'am."*** He taps his temple. ***"You're very clever Mrs. Regis. I like that in a woman."***

Karen doesn't appreciate this macho attitude. But she bites her tongue. Sergeant Olsen addresses Paul. ***"I think someone wanted your file specifically. The Doc tells me you're a lawyer?"*** Paul nods. ***"Would any of your clients know that you were seeing Doctor Shay?"***

Paul is somewhat stumped but provide the sergeant with his best answer, ***"Well, I guess anyone of them could have followed me or something, but for God's sake, I can't imagine why?"***

Sergeant Olsen asks, ***"Maybe somebody didn't like how you handled their case? Or, your fee?"*** The Sergeant chuckles at his own police humor.

Paul is bewildered and asks, ***"So, what if you're right? So, what? I mean, what the hell would anyone want with my file?"***

Sergeant Olsen says, ***"Never underestimate the criminal mind Mr. Regis. The bottom-line is, now they know a lot of personal information about you. Where you live, the fact that you're married. There's lots of reasons to collect personal information on someone. It all depends on 'motive'."*** Sergeant Olsen gets a serious look on his face. ***"It's better to be safe than sorry, right?"***

Karen becomes concerned***. "So, if I'm reading you right... You think that Paul and I might be in some sort of danger?"***

Sergeant Olsen shrugs. ***"Danger, smanger, who knows? I'm just trying to find out why that file was the only one taken."***

Paul is concerned, ***"Assuming the worst case scenario, what should we do?"***

Sergeant Olsen says, ***"For the moment, nothing. Just relax. But if anything, and I MEAN anything, out of the ordinary happens, I want you to contact me."*** He hands Paul his business card. ***"I'd also like permission to tap your home and office phones."***

Paul replies with a sense of conviction, "You can tap the home phone but I'm against involving anything to do with my clients, or the firm, at this point. I would need to clear that with our senior partner first!"

The Sergeant raises his eyebrows and shrugs as if to say, 'OK, whatever.'

Then Sergeant Olsen adds, "OK. I'm going to post a man outside for a few days though. Just until all of this blows over." Paul nods. Then the sergeant adds***, "It'll probably turn out to be nothing. A coincidence or something?"*** The Sergeant smiles. Paul and Karen smile nervously back.

Later that night

Karen and Paul are in bed. Karen has her arms around Paul. Paul has a concerned look on his face.

Karen asks, ***"Are you as worried about all of this; as I am?"***

Paul smiles and pats her arm. ***"I'm sure everything will turn out to be just fine."*** Karen closes her eyes and snuggles close to Paul. We see by Paul's expression, that he isn't altogether sure he believes what he's just told her.

 # - "Unbridled"

Westside Hospital – later that week

Doctor Shay is walking down the hall with a clip board. He pauses to write something down. The Female Doctor he spoke with at lunch a few days before, steps up to him.

The female doctor says, ***"Hi, Michael."***

Doctor Shay's train of thought is broken for a moment as he looks up at the woman and smiles. "Oh hi, Doreen. How are you?"

The female doctor responds, ***"As well as can be expected, considering this madhouse."***

Michael chuckles, then asks, ***"Say, I was curious..."***

The female doctor hooks her arm into his, and they walk together a bit. Then she asks, ***"How's that SS officer of yours doing?"***

Doctor Shay looks confused for a second. Then she clarifies, ***"The hypnosis case you were telling Doctor Hausmann and me about?"*** She obviously has a genuine interest.

Michael answers, ***"Paul Regis? He's doing good. Together we're compiling some very interesting data."***

She has to go her own way and begins to separate from Doctor Shay's arm. But before disappearing down the corridor she adds, ***"Well. I wish you both the best! I know Hausmann seemed to be intrigued, I for one am not inclined to believe that sort of stuff."***

Then she adds almost as an afterthought, as she gets further and further away from him, ***"No offense Michael."*** She waves goodbye over her shoulder, and Michael is left there standing in the hallway pondering something she said about Doctor Hausmann's interest.

The Hospital Cafeteria

Doctor Shay is standing in line with a plastic tray picking out the things he will eat for lunch. He is too busy looking around the cafeteria, and not paying attention to what's going on. One of the female servers becomes impatient.

The food server asks, ***"Mashed potatoes or rice?"***

Michael finally acknowledges her, ***"Uh, excuse me?"***

The food server repeats her questions, ***"You want the potatoes or the rice?"***

Michael finally answers, ***"Uh... rice will be fine."***

Doctor Shay arrives at the end of the line by the cash register. He pays his bill and moves through the crowded cafeteria, scanning the crowd.

He spots Doreen (the Female Doctor) and a nurse sitting at a table across the room. He makes his way over to the table and asks, ***"May I join you ladies?"***

The Nurse begins to gather her things up, and as she stands she says, ***"Sorry I have to run, I've got surgery in an hour. Enjoy. See you later Doreen."***

Doreen gestures with her hand for Michael to take a seat. Michael smiles at the departing nurse as he takes a seat across from Doreen.

Michael speaks up, ***"I hope I'm not chasing you off?"***

The nurse comments over her shoulder, ***"No, no. I'm scheduled for the O.R. in an hour. Got to run."***

Doreen is searching for something in her scrubs with one hand while managing to wave goodbye at the Nurse with the other.

Doctor Shay is curious about what Doreen is fishing for as he watches her withdraw an almost crushed cigarette package. She extracts a single bent smoke from the pack.

Michael smiles, ***"Doreen are you kidding me? You know, you should really make an appointment with me about those. I could help you quit those damned things."***

Doreen laughs and says, ***"Yea, Nasty Habit, I know. Here I am a Doctor, trying to keep my patients healthy, and I'm hooked on these damned things!"***

Doctor Shay adds, "The Plumber's pipes all leak, right?" Doreen laughs in agreement.

Michael asks, ***"Say, I, uh, I was wondering about something you said earlier."*** Doreen acknowledges his potential question with her eyes. He continues, ***"You mentioned that Doctor***

Hausmann seemed highly interested in the Regis case?"

Doreen is curious and answers, ***"Yea, he appeared to be very interested."***

Michael asks, ***"Can you remember anything specific about what he said?"***

Doreen can see by Michael's face that something is up, and her curiosity is aroused. "Is there something wrong Michael?

Michael smiles, trying to defuse his questioning. ***"No, no. I'm just interested in my peers' opinions. That's all."*** He laughs before continuing his train of thought, ***"It's just nice to have someone with credentials, validate my efforts once in a while. Everyone else around here seems to think I'm practicing Voodoo or something."*** Michael and Doreen share a laugh. Then Michael presses his point, ***"So, uh, what'd he have say?"***

Doreen looks at her watch and then starts to gather her things. Then she casually adds, ***"Nothing really, he just mentioned that he lost some relatives in a concentration camp during the war, and he wanted to know what your patient might know about that?"***

She stands up then she adds, ***"He wondered if your research might produce some historical information."*** She leans over closer to Michael's face. ***"I told him, that I thought you were***

both grasping at straws... no offense. Look, I've got to run, OK?"

Michael smiles and adds, ***"Yeah, I'll see you later. Oh, and thanks Doreen."***

Close-up of Doctor Shay's face as he begins to ponder the conversation he had with Doreen and Doctor Hausmann a week or so ago. He tries to reply that conversation.

Doreen said, ***"That's very interesting Michael. And you say there's facts?"***

Michael said, ***"Yes. There's no question that these events occurred. Herr Goltz lived. In fact, he was a major element in creating the holocaust." He pauses. "Goltz was some sort of protégé to Mengele."***

And Doctor Hausmann asked, ***"And you're absolutely sure beyond a shadow of a doubt?"***

Michael remembers answering, ***"Yes. I have copies of documents dating back to the organization of the concentration camps."***

Michael recalls looking back and forth between Doreen and Hausmann during that exchange. He also remembers telling Hausmann, ***"I can't prove that Paul didn't deliberately or unintentionally see some historical documents before. It's possible that he did, although I seriously doubt it."***

Doctor Hausmann asked, ***"Paul?"***

Doctor Shay is deep in thought as he hastily answers. ***"Yes. Paul Regis, my patient."***

Doreen interrupts, ***"Oh, oh. Aren't you violating patient confidentiality, Michael?"***

"Aren't you violating patient confidentiality, Michael?" Her voice echo's in Michael's mind, and then trails off. ***"Aren't you violating patient confidentiality, Michael?"***

We are brought back to the reality of the cafeteria; we see an almost shocked look on Michael's face. He speaks, out loud. ***"Oh my God. It's Hausmann... of course!"*** He pauses, thinking about the possible implications. He thinks to himself, 'Oh, my God.'

Doctor Shay pulls out his cell phone and dials. Through the receiver we hear the first ring.

Paul's Office

Barbara answers, ***"Good afternoon, Law Offices."*** She pauses. ***"I'll check to see if he's in Doctor Shay, please hold."***

Paul is at his desk, his intercom buzzes. He reaches up, without looking, and presses the switch. ***"Yes?"***

Barbara announces, ***"I have Doctor Shay on line three."***

Paul answers, "Thank you Barbara." He punches line three on his telephone and says, ***"Hello, Michael. What's up doc?"***

Michael is fishing and he asks, ***"I need a little information, Paul. Are you busy?"***

Paul says, ***"Well things around here are always busy, but you sound serious, what's up?"***

Michael tries to explain without revealing too much, ***"I, uh, I was hoping to ask you in person, Paul. My office? That is, if, you can get away."***

Paul is a bit surprised, but Doctor Shay's voice has a sense of urgency in it. He answers, ***"Sure, I guess so. What time?"***

Michael answers, ***"I've got a few things to do in the next couple of hours, but how about four or four-thirty?"***

Paul answers, ***"Fine. I'll see you at four."***

Doctor Shay hangs up. He walks out into the hospital corridor, takes the elevator down to the main floor and walks up to the main desk.

The Receptionist asks, ***"May I help you Doctor?"***

Michael asks, ***"Uh, yes... I was wondering if you could connect me with the personnel office."***

The receptionist smiles, reaches for a white telephone, dials, and hands the receiver to Doctor Shay. ***"Yes, this is Doctor Michael Shay. I was wondering if you could tell me if Doctor Josef Hausmann is in the hospital?"***

The woman in personnel, looks something up on the computer screen. She says, ***"I don't have Doctor Hausmann scheduled for today, but I can page him if you'd..."***

She's interrupted by another Doctor who is standing near her desk. She adds, ***"Uh, just a moment Doctor Shay, I have Doctor Hausmann's associate standing here and he wants to speak with you."*** She hands the receiver to Doctor Willet. ***"Hello. Doctor Shay? I'm Doctor Willet. I'm Doctor Hausmann's colleague? Maybe I can be of some service?"***

Doctor Shay responds, ***"Possibly. I was wondering if Doctor Hausmann was in the hospital today?"***

Doctor Willet explains, ***"No, as a matter of fact, he's home in bed with the flu today."***

Doctor Shay looking a little worried. ***"Oh, I see."***

Doctor Willet asks, ***"Is there anything I can do for you?"*** He waits for Doctor Shay to answer, but no response. ***"Maybe I can pass on a message?"***

Michael asks, ***"Uh, look I'd like to speak with him. Would it be possible for you to give me his home number?"***

Doctor Willet says, ***"I guess I can do that, hang on a second while I see if I have his home number." There's a pause, and then Doctor Willet says, "Sorry all I have is his answering service."***

Then he thanks Doctor Willet, ***"Look, Doctor Willet, I really appreciate you trying to help, thanks."*** There's a small pause while Doctor Willet acknowledges Doctor Shay's appreciation. He closes by saying, ***"Yea you too. And thanks again."***

Doctor Shay reaches over the counter and hands the woman the receiver. ***"Thank you."*** She smiles, and he walks away down the Hospital corridor, deep in thought. He walks over to a waiting area, takes a seat, and digs out his cell phone. asks, "Hey Siri". A female's robotic voice comes on, ***"Uh huh?"***

Michael asks, ***"Can you get me an address for a Doctor Josef Hausmann in Oakland California."***

Siri has found a likely person. "I have a J. Hausmann on Skyline Blvd. in Oakland, California. Would you like a telephone number?"

Doctor Shay smiles. He says***, "Yes please"*** Siri shows him the phone number on his cell phone, then she asks him, ***"Would you like me to call that number for you?"***

Michael says, ***"Yes please."***

His cell phone begins to ring. Once. Twice and then... ***"This is Joseph Hausmann."***

Michael asks, ***"Doctor Hausmann?"***

Visiting the Hausmann's home

He's cruising slowly, reading all of the numbers on the houses. He stops in front of the Hausmann home, confirms the box number, then pulls into the driveway and parks. He gets out and presses the doorbell.

Mrs. Hausmann walks to the front door to answer it. Doctor Shay is standing there waiting. The door swings open and the woman says, ***"Yes, can I help you young man?"***

Michael inquires, ***"Mrs. Hausmann?"***

Mrs. Hausmann smiles. ***"Yes?"***

Doctor Shay answers, ***"I'm Doctor Shay, from West Side Hospital? I'm a co-worker of your husband's. I was wondering if I could disturb him."*** She frowns and looks a bit confused. Michael adds, ***"I realize he's ill, so I'll keep my visit brief."***

Mrs. Hausmann thinks about his request for a pregnant pause before answering, ***"I guess that would be alright Doctor Shay,"*** She opens the front door and tells Michael, ***"Please come in. If you don't mind can you please wait in the living room? I'll let my husband know that you're here."*** Michael nods, and enters the Hausmann home. He makes his way into the living room and finds a couch to sit on.

Mrs. Hausmann says, ***"I must tell you Doctor Shay, I'm a little confused?"***

Michael asks, ***"Why is that mame?"***

Mrs. Hausmann answers, ***"You said that my husband was ill?"*** Doctor Shay nods. Then she asks, ***"Who told you that?"***

Michael tries to explain, ***"I spoke with your husband's associate, Doctor Willet. He said your husband was home with the flu."***

She patronizes him with a smile and then reaches for a telephone on a small end table. Then she addresses Doctor Shay, ***"Please excuse me for a moment."***

Doctor Shay nods and remains seated while she makes her call. ***"Yes, hello. This is Mrs. Hausmann; may I speak with my husband – Doctor Josef Hausmann please?"***

She pauses. Doctor Shay is a little confused. Then Michael hears her say, ***"I see... uh, no, that won't be necessary, thank you."***

She hangs up and turns towards Doctor Shay. ***"Well, it appears that my husband is playing hooky Doctor."***

Michael is beginning to get a bit confused. He says, ***"I see."***

Mrs. Hausmann is quite confused. She says, ***"I don't know what's going on here Doctor Shay, but I would know if my husband was home ill. I can tell you that he is not!"***

This information puts Doctor Shay deeper in thought. He's confused. The silence is broken by the sounds of someone entering the house. A young man stands in the archway of the living room.

Russell Hausmann steps into the living room. He says, ***"Hi mom."***

Mrs. Hausmann makes an introduction, ***"Russell, this is Doctor Shay. He apparently works at the same hospital as your father."***

Doctor Shay nods. Russell crosses the room and shakes hands with the Doctor. Russel says, ***"Glad to meet you Doctor Shay. So, you work with my father?"***

Michael corrects the misunderstanding, ***"No. I don't actually work with your dad, I just work at the same hospital, but yes your father and I know each other."***

Mrs. Hausmann asks, ***"Russell? Did your father mention anything to you about going someplace other than his office, or the hospital, today?"***

Russell is thinking momentarily. Doctor Shay interrupts.

Michael asks, ***"If you don't mind me asking, do you recall your dad mentioning the name, Paul Regis? Or Herman Goltz?"***

Russell says, ***"Uh let's see, Goltz, Goltz. That name sounds familiar. He pauses. Then he has an epiphany. "Yes, Goltz, of course! I saw a picture of that man in my father's photo album."***

Doctor Shay is surprised, and Mrs. Hausmann's expression changes to bewilderment. Mrs. Hausmann is shocked. ***"You went into your father's things, Russell?"***

Russell answers quickly, ***"No, of course not. I simply interrupted him looking at a photo album last night. I went ahead and asked about the photographs, that's all."***

Michael interrupts, ***"Russell, would it be possible for me to have a look at that photo album?"***

Mrs. Hausmann immediately interrupts, ***"I don't understand Doctor Shay."***

Michael tries to explain, ***"Mrs. Hausmann, look. There are a lot of unanswered questions that I'm trying desperately to answer. Maybe a look at your husband's photo album will help?"***

Russell is understandably concerned, ***"I'm sorry but I don't understand what's going on here, will someone please explain? Is my father in trouble in some way?"***

Mrs. Hausmann doesn't understand either and looks towards Doctor Shay for a reasonable explanation.

Michael tries to explain, ***"I have reason to believe that your father..."*** He looks at Mrs. Hausmann. ***"Your husband..."*** He pauses. ***"He may be involved in something very dangerous."***

Mrs. Hausmann is now very concerned and says, ***"I'm sure that you're mistaken Doctor Shay."***

Michael answers, ***"What if I'm correct about this, wouldn't you want an opportunity to help ensure that your husband comes out of this alive?"*** He pauses. ***"If I can find something in that photo book, maybe I can clear up a few things? It may even clear your husband, who knows? Otherwise..."*** He pauses. ***"I'm going to have to go to the police."***

Mrs. Hausmann looks very worried now. Russell speaks, ***"Look, Doctor Shay, I don't know what's going on but if it'll help my father I'll show you the book."***

Mrs. Hausmann reluctantly agrees, ***"I suppose it couldn't hurt."***

Michael smiles and says, ***"Thank you. Believe me, I have only the best of intentions."***

Russell starts to head upstairs, ***"Come on, I'll show you."*** All three of them climb the stairs headed for the Hausmann study.

The upstairs study.

They enter. Russell starts to rummage through his father's desk. He says, ***"Well, it was right here on top of his desk, last night?"***

Mrs. Hausmann crosses the room and goes directly to a drawer below the wall bookshelf. She opens it and withdraws the album. She holds it close to herself for a moment (almost hugging it) and then she turns, and hands it to Doctor Shay. She says, ***"My husband spends hours looking at this damn thing."***

The Doctor, sensing that this photo album is a key element to the Hausmann family. He carefully takes it from Mrs Hausmann gently.

He walks over to the desk, takes a seat in Josef's chair, and opens it. Russell steps closer to looks over the Doctor's shoulder.

Mrs. Hausmann walks to a chair across from them and sits down. Apparently she wants nothing to do with the book.

In many ways Doctor Shay is starting to realize that Josef still lives in the world that this book represents. As Doctor Shay begins to scan the photographs and newspaper articles in the album, he pauses and looks up at Mrs. Hausmann. He is at a loss for words. She senses this, and tries to explain, ***"Often I'd ask Josef why he kept that thing? He would always say, 'So I do not forget'."***

Russell interrupts, pointing to a photograph in the album. ***"That's is a photograph of my father and his parents. My grandparents. My grandparents were killed by the Nazi's."***

Doctor Shay sympathizes with Russel. He looks at the photograph, then turns the page. On the net page he asks Russell, ***"Who is this?"***

Russell leans over and points to an old newspaper photograph, before saying, "That's Goltz, the man you asked about. He killed my grandparents. In fact, he ran that particular concentration camp and was responsible for killing thousands of Jews. My father told me that he was like Satan himself."

Michael looks at Russell and asks***, "Your Father told you that?"***

Russell adds, ***"Yes, he said Goltz shot them both in cold blood."***

Doctor Shay looks at Mrs. Hausmann and asks, ***"Has your husband appeared somewhat depressed lately?"***

Mrs. Hausmann says, ***"Well, he hasn't been sleeping well... and, uh... now that you mention it, he has seemed a little pre-***

occupied. He kept saying that he has a lot of hospital business on his mind and cited that as the culprit for his sleeplessness."

Michael interrupts Mrs. Hausmann, "Mrs. Hausmann?" Mrs. Hausmann's train of thought is broken, and she looks at Doctor Shay. He asks, ***"Does your husband own a gun?"***

Mrs. Hausmann smiles and begins to shake her head laughing. Then she adds, ***"Doctor Shay... I can assure you that before my husband thinks about committing suicide, I would know about it."***

Michael is serious and says, ***"I'm not suggesting suicide, Mrs. Hausmann."*** Mrs. Hausmann is shocked that Doctor Shay could be suggesting something even worse. ***"I think I resent your accusation Doctor. You come into my house, a perfect stranger, and insinuate that my husband is going to what? Commit murder? Really! Is that what this is all about?"*** Mrs. Hausmann is angry at this point, and ready to ask the Doctor to leave.

Michael almost pleads at this point, ***"If I'm wrong and believe me Mrs. Hausmann I hope that I am... then I'll accept the responsibility of what I'm suggesting."*** Michael pauses for a moment. ***"Do you know where he keeps it?"***

Mrs. Hausmann, at this point, is shocked at Doctor Shay's brazen attitude. Trying to protect her husband, she says, ***"I don't think that's any of your business, sir."***

Russell speaks up, ***"Mother! What if he's right? What then?"***

Mrs. Hausmann shakes her head "no", refusing to believe any of this. Russell turns towards Doctor Shay and takes command of the situation, ***"Come on, I'll show it to you."***

The two men leave the study and Doctor Shay follows Russell into the Hausmann's master bedroom. Russell goes to the nightstand on his father's side of the bed. He opens the second drawer, it appears empty, he slides his hand all over the interior of the drawer trying to feel for the gun. He stops, looks at Doctor Shay, then slightly panic stricken he opens the top drawer and inspects it. He reaches in and removes a half empty box of 9mm ammunition, looks at it for a moment then hands it to Doctor Shay. He is scared and sad about the implications.

Russell says, ***"It's gone. Now what?"***

Michael tries to be positive. He says, ***"I think it's important that no one panics... let's give your father the benefit of a doubt, all right? May I have permission to look around your father's study? Maybe he just moved it in there?"***

Russell, somewhat disappointed in his father's decisions, waves him on. The two men return to the study, Mrs. Hausmann is still sitting in the chair, waiting patiently for good news. Russell carefully crosses the room and places a comforting hand on her shoulder, she reaches up and clasps it with her own... knowing full well that the news isn't looking too good.

Russell asks his mom, ***"The gun?"*** She's silent. Then he adds, ***"It's gone, Doctor Shay was right."***

Doctor Shay is rummaging through several drawers in Mr. Hausmann's desk. He's becoming very worried, and finally says, ***"Well, I was hoping that some kind of mistake happened, and we'd find his gun."*** He pauses. ***"But I'm sorry to say that there can be no mistake. His gun is definitely missing."***

Just then, Doctor Shay spots the Paul Regis file folder in a pile of papers on Doctor Hausmann's desk. He is shocked and says***, "This is my client's file. It was stolen last week from my office during a burglary."***

Mrs. Hausmann cups her forehead with her hand. She begins to break down crying. Russell immediately goes over to comfort his mom. Now she realizes the severity of the situation.

Russell is now mentally behind Doctor Shay and wants to help. He asks***, "So, what's the plan?"***

Michael speculates. ***"Here's what I think. I think that your father has concluded that my***

patient, Paul Regis, is really Herr Goltz - reincarnated. The man that murdered his parents." He pauses. ***"He's not of course! The real Goltz died a few years before Paul was even born."*** He can see that Russell and Mrs. Hausmann are a little confused about all of this. He knows that this needs a better explanation, but there simply isn't time to do that right now. He says, ***"Look I can't explain now... we've got to locate your father before he does something he'll regret!"***

Russell and Mrs. Hausmann nod "yes" simultaneously. Doctor Shay grabs his cell phone and dials. Then he looks at the Hausmann's, ***"I'm sorry but you'll just have to trust me for a little while longer!"*** His phone is ringing. ***"Metro Police, Sergeant Olsen speaking."***

"Sergeant Olsen? This is Michael Shay... fine, fine, uh... look, I located the missing Paul Regis file." Pauses while the facts sink in. ***"No, no. I found it in the desk drawer of a Doctor Josef Hausmann. Yes. Doctor Josef Hausmann. He works at West Side Hospital."*** He pauses. ***"I think he's planning to kill Paul Regis!"***

Law Offices

We see the telephone ring. Barbara's hand reaches over to answer. ***"Good afternoon, Law Offices."*** Pauses. ***"No, I'm sorry, Doctor***

Shay. He said he was going out to take care of some personal business, and then he mentioned that he would be off to see you." She pauses. ***"No, sir... he didn't tell me. Is something wrong?"*** She pauses. ***"Yes, I will. Yes, sure, I understand."***

Doctor Shay is sitting at Josef's desk, he slowly hangs up. He looks defeated, ***"Goddammit. He's already left the office, SHIT!"***

The Hausmann Living Room

We see Russell, Mrs. Hausmann and Doctor Shay. The doorbell rings and Russell goes over and let's Sergeant Olsen in. The first thing Sargent Olson does is ask, ***"I take it, he didn't show up?"***

Michael says, ***"No. Nothing."***

Sargent Olsen asks, ***"You the Hausmann son?"*** Russell nods. Olsen looks at Doctor Shay. ***"Ok, here's what I want you to do. You and the kid go to your office, see if you can intercept Regis there. If you do, take him to some public place close by, away from your office, and call me to let me know where you ended up."*** He pauses. ***"In the meantime, I'm gonna run over to the Regis place, maybe I can catch him there?"***

With the meeting breaking up, Sargent Olsen remembers Mrs. Hausmann. ***"Oh, uh, Mrs. Hausmann. I'm placing an officer outside in***

case your husband returns, alright? Please keep him here if he shows up?"

She begins to cry, and Olsen lays a gentle hand on her shoulder. ***"Look, uh, I'll handle this as gently as your husband allows me to, alright? I promise. But it's up to him, OK?"*** She tries to smile and nods that she understands the situation.

Russell interrupts, ***"Everything will be fine Mom, you'll see."*** He kisses her on the cheek. Doctor Shay and Sargent Olsen leave the house.

Downtown

We see Paul Regis window shopping. He has a small package under his arm. He stops at a window and pauses, looking at something in the display.

In the reflection in the glass, he spots the man with the beard across the street. As he turns to look, a bus passes by obscuring his view.

When the bus passes, Paul notices that the man is gone! He is a little concerned, but shrugs his shoulders, looks at his watch and recalls his appointment with Doctor Shay.

Paul is whistling to the radio in his car as he drives to Doctor Shay's office for his appointment.

"Action Theme"

Dr. Shay's Office

Paul pulls up to the curb directly in front of Doctor Shay's office. He steps out of the car, standing there for a moment straightening his coat.

The front of a car across the street sits another car with Josef Hausmann sitting at the wheel. Paul is still standing alongside his vehicle. We hear the engine rev up in the Hausmann vehicle. And suddenly the vehicle lunges forward, headed straight for Paul. Paul has obviously become the "prime target."

Paul begins to walk towards the front door of Doctor Shay's office building.

Josef Hausmann's face is filled with hate, he slowly smiles as he realizes that HE is in c0ontrol of the situation. He guns the motor as the vehicle picks up speed. The car squeals it's tires as it heads straight for Paul who is unaware of everything that is going on.

At the last possible moment Paul looks in his car and smiles. He opens the door and leans into his car, reaching into the back seat for the package he held earlier.

It's just out of reach as he crawls deeper into the vehicle to get it. He hears the approaching car at the last minute and has just enough time to yank his leg inside as the speeding vehicle tears off his door. The offending car continues on its way down the street disappearing in city traffic.

Paul is visibly shaken but in a fit of anger climbs out of the car standing in the street as he watches the speeding vehicle disappear.

Paul realizes that the occupant won't be able to hear him, he goes ahead and yells! ***"You fucking asshole!"***

The front door to Doctor Shay's office opens and Doctor Shay followed by Russell Hausmann come running outside to find a very irritated Paul Regis.

Michael speaks up first, ***"Are you alright?"***

Paul vents, ***"Can you believe that stupid bastard? He damned near killed me! Oh God, look at my car, will ya look at that?"***

Paul is heartbroken about his car and is hardly aware of Doctor Shay and Russell's presence.

Russel speaks up, ***"It was no accident, Mr. Regis."***

Michael interrupts, ***"Paul, this is Russell Hausmann. He's the son of the man who just tried to kill you."***

Paul is utterly bewildered. He's flabbergasted, and asks, ***"Why does he want to kill me?"***

Michael doesn't answer his question but instead grabs Paul by the shoulder and says, "Come on, were taking you to a safe place! I'll explain on the way."

The three men walk around the building to the parking lot out back, and the three of them get into Doctor Shay's car. They emerge out of the driveway next to Doctor Shay's Office and pass Paul's smashed car (Paul takes another look at the damage), and they drive down the street away from Doctor Shay's office.

From an alley across the street, we spot Josef Hausmann's vehicle hiding between two office buildings. Josef Hausmann spots the three men in Doctor Shay's vehicle as it passes by and he starts his motor, pulling out into traffic, following Doctor Shay's vehicle.

A Local Restaurant

The three men enter the bar area and take seats at a small table.

Michael is just finishing up the explanation of what has transpired with regards to Josef Hausmann, ***"So, you see, Doctor Hausmann thinks that you're Herman Goltz, reincarnated."***

Paul says, ***"Well in a manner of speaking I guess I am?"***

Michael corrects Paul, ***"Were. Past tense. That was a long, long time ago."*** H4 pauses. He can see that Paul is very shaken. ***"Look, you have no control over what happened in the past. It goes without saying then, that you cannot be held responsible for things you may have done when you were on this Earth***

as Herr Goltz. If indeed, you really were Goltz."

Russell smiles and tries to comfort Paul. "All of this is kind of hard for me to swallow to Mr. Regis, but I'm sure the Doctor's right. It's my father that needs to be set straight."

Paul is shocked as he stares off into space. He says, ***"I had no idea things would get this far, out of hand."***

Michael, feeling somewhat guilty, announces, "I'm sorry that I got you into all of this Paul."

Paul smiles and looks at Doctor Shay, knowing that he inadvertently may have made Doctor Shay feel guilty. ***"Look, Michael. It was my decision, alright?"***

Russell interrupts, ***"Doctor Shay, shouldn't we contact Sargent Olsen?"*** Calling Sergeant Olsen had slipped both of their minds, with all the excitement.

Michael immediately responds, ***"Yes, yes. By all means!"***

He pulls out his cell phone and looks up Olsen's contact information and places the call. As he does Russell excuses himself to use the restroom.

#7 - "Uplifting Escapades

From the rear parking lot of the restaurant, we see Josef Hausmann walking closer and closer to the back door.

The door opens and Hausmann enters a small hallway. A man steps from the restroom glances up, and in fear for his life, backs into the doorway he just emerged from.

Hausmann continues down the hall and around the corner until he is in the main part of the restaurant.

Many people are relaxing as they're drinking and visiting with each other. The noise level is fairly loud. Hausmann raises his hand, and there's a handgun in it. A female patron sees the gun first, and she starts screaming... HE'S GOT A GUN!.

The crowd panics and clears a path leaving a clear isle between the Hausmann, his pistol and the table where Paul, Doctor Shay, and Russell are sitting.

All conversation comes to a dead stop. Doctor Shay notices Hausmann first. He speaks, "Oh, my God." He holds out his two outstretched arms and tries to reason with Doctor Hausmann, "Josef, please... don't do this."

Josef lifts the pistol and points it directly at Paul, as he speaks to Doctor Shay, ***"I'm warning you Michael, do not intervene. This is family business!"***

Doctor Shay slowly walks from behind the seated Paul Regis, and carefully places himself slightly in front of Paul. He adds, "Josef, please. Listen to me. This man is innocent." The man you want is dead, a long, long, time ago! This is not..."

● ● ● BLAM ● ● ●

A single shot rings out, interrupting Doctor Shay's speech and sending him flying back onto Paul's lap.

Paul catches Michael as he attempts to keep Doctor Shay from falling to the floor, but Michael's body weight and the momentum from the shot send him tumbling over backwards as well.

Michael rolls over and away from Paul, and Paul stands up, holding his hands in front of himself gesturing for Doctor Hausmann to stop.

Josef's hand reestablishes a bead onto Paul with his pistol, his hand is trembling, and he begins to understand for a brief moment that he's just shot the wrong human being.

Paul sizes up the situation and starts to move away from the tipped over table. Hausmann sees this and snaps the gun back up towards Paul.

Josef yells***, "No, Herr Goltz! You shall not escape this time!"***

Paul stops, he's petrified with fear, he's ridged. Michael Shay moans, moving a little on the floor; Paul sneaks a small glance and is somewhat relieved that Michael is not already dead.

Russell Hausmann re-enters the room from the back restroom, slowly at first and then he walks closer to the standing Paul Regis. Then he begins pleading with his father, ***"Dad? Dad, please. Don't do this. This man is not Herr Goltz, he's innocent. Herr Goltz died before Mr. Regis was even born."***

Josef all but ignores his son's words and he yells, ***"He's a butcher!"***

He lifts his other arm to help steady his shooting arm, and he takes a bead on Paul. ***"He murdered my Parents!"***

Russell immediately tries to shield Paul saying, ***"No, Dad... you're wrong! Herr Goltz murdered grandpa and grandma, not this man!"***

Josef seems to become more angry. He yells at Russell, ***"Shut up! Move away! I shall not hear such things from a son of mine! This is not your affair!"***

Russell attempts to speak again and the elder Hausmann says, ***"Not another word!"*** Josef moves closer to Paul. He has an insane look on his face. He adds, "Move away from him, Russell."

Russell doesn't move right away, he looks at Paul, frustrated that there is nothing he can do. Josef repeats his command, ***"Move. NOW!"***

Russell is startled by his father's determination, and he backs away from the table.

Paul begins pleading for his life, ***"Please... Mr. Hausmann, I'm innocent... I didn't even know about Herr Goltz until a few weeks ago, you're going to kill an innocent man, please..."***

The elder Hausmann takes another step closer; he cocks the pistol, taking care that he will not miss when he does shoot.

Josef says, ***"Yes. Go ahead Herr Goltz, beg me. Beg for your life like the people you slaughtered at the camp. Beg like my parents did. Beg me."***

Paul tries one last time, ***"Please? Mr. Hausmann, don't do this."***

Josef is drawn back in time to that day when the real Herman Goltz slaughtered his parents. Josef seems to be caught up in the moment, as he raves, ***"The women, the little children, all-crying for their lives... They were begging you for mercy. Remember, how I begged you?"***

Paul adds, ***"Doctor Hausmann, I'm Paul Regis, I've never even been to Germany, I never knew Herr Goltz, I swear."***

Josef has finally heard Paul say something, but he isn't buying it, ***"LIAR !"*** Hausmann smiles. ***"Now I want you to look around the room Herr Goltz, go ahead... Take a final look."***

He waves the barrel of the pistol in a little circle, and looks around the restaurant before saying, ***"These are the last things you will ever see...EVER!"***

He lifts the pistol once again as if he's about to fire. He adds, ***"May your soul, ROT IN HELL!"***

Just then a voice comes from behind Hausmann. It's Sargent Olsen. "Put the gun down Doctor Hausmann."

Hausmann is surprised but doesn't move a muscle. Olsen repeats his command again***. "I mean it doctor! Do yourself and your family a favor and put the gun down."*** Olsen grips his revolver tighter, realizing that he might have to kill someone today. He doesn't want to, but...

Olsen tries to beat some sense into Hausmann one more time***, "Doctor Hausmann, please do as I say. I'm Sergeant Olsen from the Metropolitan Police Department. Please put the gun down on the floor and step backwards towards me."*** He pauses. ***"The last thing I want to do is kill you, but if you do not put that gun down immediately, I'll be forced to shoot."***

He pauses for Hausmann's response. Josef says, ***"I have a responsibility."***

Hausmann starts to lower the gun a little, pauses for a moment, and then lifts the gun again. Russell Hausmann sees that his father is going to shoot an innocent man; he makes the decision to step in front of Paul. The elder Hausmann pulls the trigger twice.

• • • BLAM • • •

• • • BLAM • • •

Two shots are fired, Russell falls to the floor from his father's shot and the elder Hausmann is shot by the Sergeant.

#8 - "Nobel Ventures"

Immediately Sergeant Olsen runs to the elder Hausmann, kicks the gun away and reaches down to feel his pulse. He looks up at Paul who is frozen stiff with fear, Olsen shakes his head no.

Olsen walks across the room towards Paul, he looks over at the bartender who is just standing there with eyes as big as silver dollars, he puts his gun away and looks over at the frozen bartender. "Well? Call 911!"

The bartended rushes to complete his command.

He hastily crosses the remaining space, leaning down to check Russell first for a pulse. There isn't one.

Michael moans, and Olsen looks over knowing now that at least Doctor Shay is alive. He sucks air between his teeth in a snapping sound and stands back up. He looks at Paul. ***"How 'bout you? You alright?"***

Paul is still dazed, but he has the wherewithal to nod. When he finally gets a hold of himself, he helps Olsen to help Doctor Shay to his feet.

Paul asks, ***"Michael?"*** Doctor Shay tries to smile but ends up grimacing with pain.

Olsen says, ***"Take it easy, Doc... an ambulance is on the way."***

Michael can see Russell Hausmann laying on the floor. He inquires, ***"What about Russell?"***

Sergeant Olsen closes his eyes and shakes his head no. Doctor Shay struggles to speak to Paul. ***"Ironic, isn't it?"*** Paul listens as Doctor Shay continues, ***"One Hausmann tries to take your life, while another... saves it."***

Michael is very emotional, and he tears up. Then he adds, ***"Who knows? Maybe next time around, you can save Russell's life?"***

Karen Regis runs into the front door of the restaurant, she comes to a sliding stop. She sees Paul and Sargent Olsen holding Michael. She says, ***"Honey?"***

Paul Regis looks at her and smiles, indicating that he is all right. She's a little panic stricken and runs over to comfort him.

#9 - "Complaisance"

The End

About the Author…

DENNY MAGIC

IF YOU HAVE ANY INTEREST IN MY LIFE STORY... PLEASE VISIT MY WEBSITE AT DENNYMAGIC1.COM, AND NAVIGATE OVER TO MY "BIO" PAGE WHERE YOU CAN FIND MY 500 PAGE AUTOBIOGRAPHY.

Made in the USA
Middletown, DE
26 January 2025

70260800R00086